Chasing Angels
And Failing Aristotle

By Michael Sinnes

Volume 2
Renaissance Mind

To Cat,

Every time I hear the song "Centerfold" by the J Gyles Band I think of you, and my blood runs cold.

Then He said to Thomas, "Put your finger here; see my hands. Reach out your hand and put it into my side. Stop doubting and believe."

John 20:27

Failing Aristotle

Easy

We broke up. Yeah, it was tough. I'll admit that I was crushed by what Jessica did to me. There was a long period of wasting my time wondering where I went wrong. I wasn't afraid of moving on. Instead, I held on to the hope that everything may one day work out. In the end, however, moving on was a hell of a lot easier than I ever thought it would be. One day I was just over her. I owed all that to Portia Kiddy. She was the hottest redhead I'd ever laid eyes on – slim at the waist with an ass for days. Her profession maintained her flawless physique. She was a yoga instructor by day and a dancer by night. I went to her yoga class anytime I could. No matter what I always worked hard to do the poses right, but I wasn't going for my health. I just liked to watch her bend over in those pants. Although I tried time and again to get it on in the yoga studio, she always made me wait. I didn't think the wait was any easier for her because she was usually the one jumping my bones by the time we got home. She was definitely My Kind Of Crazy. Whenever we both had a spare moment we did everything possible to get together. Things were serious and I didn't mind at all.

I was Hard To Love. I pushed women away the second they got close to me. It wasn't uncommon for me to break up with a girl and come crawling back a few days later. Sometimes I did it on a semi-weekly basis. I'm not sure why I did it in the past, but I never tried it with Portia. I'm sure that's because I found her at one of the lowest points of my life, and she took the time to pick me up even after she said she didn't want to. She never held on too tight, and that's probably why I never ran away from her. Hell, just the thought of leaving her most mornings put a damper on the good mood brought on by waking up next to her.

I silenced the alarm as fast as possible, and I tried not to wake Portia as I got out of bed. After I got my arm out from under her I sat on the edge of the bed, trying to get the blood flowing again. It was barely eight when I looked at my phone. I had an unread text message, but I didn't have time to check it just yet. In all reality I should have woken up earlier to start working on my paper that was due in a few hours. But I wasn't worried. I never missed a deadline on a paper, and that wasn't about to change. I had my academic writing system down to a science.

Even though Portia didn't have to be to work for a while, I wasn't going to leave without saying goodbye. I gave her a shake after I was showered and dressed. "Portia," I leaned in closer to whisper in her ear. "Hey, baby."

She rolled on to her back and I helped her clear the mess of hair out of her face. "Are you leaving me?" she asked.

"'Fraid so. I gotta start heading toward The University. I've got a paper to write before class."

"I'm gonna miss you." She puckered her lips and I kissed her.

"I'm gonna miss you, too. Am I gonna see you tonight?"

"I'll call you when I get done teaching. My class is around the corner from your place."

"Can't wait," I said as I stood and pulled my backpack over my shoulders.

"Love you."

"I love you, too, Miss Kiddy." I leaned in to give her one last kiss before I walked out of the room. She was snoring by the time I got to her bedroom door.

When I was outside I checked the time again and remembered the message on my phone. Although I'm a very outgoing person when I'm in public, I tend to keep to myself in private, so I didn't get much unexpected correspondence. The message was a welcome surprise…until I saw whom it was from. I'd deleted her number long before, but there was no forgetting Jessica's number.

"Are we still on for tonight?"

She and I hadn't spoken in three months. With all the moving on I'd done in that time I'd forgotten that Jessica and I agreed to see one another again on 11-11-11, a Friday. I even requested the day off from work after Jess and I stopped speaking to make sure I'd have the night free. As a bartender, I didn't get many weekends off and I thought the Friday night off was a blessing in disguise. I'd completely forgotten the reason why I had the day off in the first place. I took another look at the three elevens on my phone. It was one of the many problems I ran into with Jessica. When Jess and I first broke up I spent most of my free time trying to finish the book I'd written for her, but I hadn't worked on it in a long time. The separation from the novel made forgetting about Jessica a lot easier, but I didn't know what to do. I promised her I'd see

2

her after three months? I owed her my life. If I made her a promise I had to keep it, right? I guess I hadn't moved on as much as I thought.

I responded while I rode the escalator down into the Chinatown Metro Station. "I'll be out of class at 2. Let me know when you're free."

I made up for all the time I hadn't spent thinking about Jessica during my trip to Tenleytown. Was she still holding on to What Might've Been like I'd done for so long? Had she broken up with her boyfriend? Did she want to leave the past behind us? Did she want to get back together? Of the millions of thoughts racing simultaneously through my head, the one that bothered me most was my inability to just say no and move on with my life. Deep down I knew I was hiding from my feelings for Jessica when I started spending more and more time with Portia. I loved Portia with all my heart, but there was still a part of me that loved Jessica, too. Although I stopped drinking myself to sleep when I started seeing Portia, I knew that sleeping with someone to fall asleep was no different than any other addiction.

When I arrived at The University metro, I walked the mile to campus to try and get my mind off Jessica and back on the task at hand. I usually made sure to allot one hour of work for every page of a paper's assigned length. The paper was supposed to be five pages. It was nine o'clock when I took my usual seat in the library basement and I only had four hours until the paper was due. If it wasn't for the fact that college was ninety-nine percent bullshit and one per cent intellect, I might have been in trouble. Most college kids in that situation would have had a meltdown, emailing the professor to beg for an extension. That's because most college kids at The University were just that, kids. They'd never experienced any real pressure, so they thought their future was over if they got a bad grade or didn't finish a paper on time. Luckily, I wrote amazing works of crap under pressure and I could've given a fuck less about the quality of work. Last time I checked, C's got degrees just as well as A's did, and people didn't buy books based on the writer's GPA.

Before you go jumping to conclusions about how well I did in school, I should tell you that I usually got B's on every paper I wrote, even the ones I wrote for other people. Yes, I was well aware of the fact that writing papers for other people was cheating, but I had good reason. When I was writing those papers, I was injured and couldn't work.

Academic Integrity took a backseat to starvation. Only those who know What It's Like can understand the necessity of moral flexibility in situations like that. In the end, I got more writing experience from cheating than most professional writers get in their first ten years of writing.

I wrote for students with all types of majors, varying from political science to physics. One kid came to me two hours before he had a ten page paper due. He was a marketing major and he had some decent notes. For two hundred bucks and an eighth ounce of weed I turned three pages of notes into an A paper with half an hour to spare (whoever said cheating doesn't pay off was a fucking moron).

Although my underground writing business kept me alive, I lost a lot of respect for the American education system. Just passing wasn't good enough for me. I wanted to learn something, and something valuable for that matter. My higher pursuit of knowledge taught me two of the most valuable lessons I've ever learned. First, I couldn't expect to learn from anyone but myself. Second, the college writing system was as formulaic as Dan Brown's writing style.

The most difficult part of the formula was the first step: coming up with both a topic *and* an argument. When college professors assigned most papers they gave a broad topic on which to write. Narrowing that topic was crucial to appropriate argument development. Scope of the topic depended upon the paper's length. Too wide of a scope and the logic surrounding the argument was too loose. Too narrow of a scope and I'd fall short of the assigned length. I solved that problem with a methodical approach to research.

Most undergraduate college papers were written based on the class's assigned readings. In those cases, selection of research materials was done for me. Unless there were twenty books on the assigned reading list, I used all of the books I could get my hands on in the library. Let me tell you, professors for the lower level classes practically gave their students the papers. To my dismay, I actually had to set aside time to write upper-level undergraduate, masters, and doctoral papers (yes, even they cheat). Although these longer, more involved papers required more effort, they were just as easy to write as a freshman paper.

Topic selection was as simple as narrowing the search field on the library's computer catalog system or journal database. Once a search yielded between ten and twenty results, I selected all the text in the search field, copied it, and pasted it into the document. Then I had a topic of the appropriate scope and a list of research materials. After I had my research materials in hand, I made sure to plan out my research before I began. I developed a mathematical tool to help me reign in the amount of time I spent researching. I multiplied the assigned page count by three to estimate the number of paragraphs I'd have to write to fill the body of the paper. This gave me an overestimation for the number of citations I had to find. Then it was just a matter of finding keywords associated with the topic. If I was looking in a journal article on the computer, it was as easy as Ctrl+F and Find Next. If I was looking in a physical journal I scanned the whole article looking for the same keywords. If I was looking through books, I looked for keywords in the Table of Contents and the index before I scanned the body of the book. No matter what media I looked through, I picked anything that looked good – and I do mean anything. I used an art writers, politicians, and press secretaries have practiced for centuries, context. As long as I used appropriate context for the argument, I could use any information to argue any point as long as the information was in line with the topic. I bullshit you not. I picked out a bunch of quotes at random, found a common theme between them, and argued a point.

Once my citations were in some logical order, all I had to do was fill in the space between. I made sure to maintain the logical sequencing from paragraph to paragraph while favoring sentence to sentence continuity over grammar. I wrote a full paragraph to make sure the argument was in line with the previous paragraph. Then I went back and adjusted the sentence to sentence flow in the previous paragraph. This seems complex, but it got easier the more I did it. I could've taught this system to a fourth grader and they could've turned out passing papers in a college class. A passing grade will get anyone a degree, and the degree was what college was all about, right?

I finished my paper that morning in record time. I got five pages out with over an hour to spare. I had time to drive home, take my pants off, roll a joint, smoke, put my pants back on, and get a snack on the way to class. I got those little, white powdered donuts and chocolate milk. I'm sure my professors knew I was always high when I went to class. I always showed up with little snacks like that.

Failing Aristotle

After I turned in the paper and took my seat, I pulled out my notebook and started writing whatever came to mind. That's how I passed my time in class. I've had trouble sitting for long periods of time since I was a kid. Marijuana helped a lot when I got old enough to start smoking it on a regular basis, but it usually wore off long before class was over. Even after my high wore off, writing in my notebook made sitting through class a lot easier. I was still paying attention to what people were saying, and it gave the appearance that I was taking copious notes. I drafted outlines for my novel; wrote poems; and even developed a theory that unified relativity, gravity, and quantum mechanics. I usually made sure to raise my head and listen to what some of the students said during the class discussion. Participation was a big part of college so I at least tried to look like I cared. Most people don't participate when they don't do the readings, but I always did. Like writing academic papers, there was a method to participating when you shouldn't be able to. I listened to what the other students had to say and derived some bullshit off their statements. I had a pretty good working knowledge of history and literary devices, so I was able to come up with a couple statements at random and squeeze them in here and there.

When class was over I checked my phone again and there were messages from both Jessica and Portia.

Jess's message read, "I'm out of class at five. We should grab Steak and Egg."

I typed "K" before I opened the message from Portia.

Hers read, "It's only noon and I'm already getting agitated. I can't wait to see you tonight."

I went home and rolled a joint to pass the time, trading dirty text messages with Portia in hopes it might lighten her mood. Portia helped me keep my mind off Jessica for nearly three months, and she did a good job that afternoon, too. I'd nearly forgotten about Jessica when she texted me to come by a little after five. I'd lost track of time talking to Portia, so I spent a few minutes getting ready before I ran out to the truck. When I got to Jessica's apartment, she already had a pre-dinner joint ready for us.

"How've you been?" she asked as she led me to the couch and lit up.

"You know, just going to school and work most days. This is the first Friday night I've had off in months. How about you?"

"Pretty much the same. I'm still working in the same restaurant and going to an internship two days a week. Anytime I'm not working or interning I'm in class or doing homework. How's the lady friend?"

"She's good. We've been seeing a lot more of each other lately. How's your future husband?"

"What makes you think I'm going to marry him?"

"I don't know if you'll marry him, but he's in the Navy. He'll ask you eventually."

She rolled her eyes at the comment. Although she never liked to admit it, she still knew I was usually right in my assessments, even if I'd never met the person I assessed. We smoked in silence for a few minutes, but that never lasted too long. She knew how much the silence bothered me, so she got the conversation going again. "It was weird not seeing you."

"It was for me, too, but I did see you once."

"Why didn't you come and say hi?"

"You were across campus and I was having a really bad day. I didn't want to drag you down when we hadn't seen each other in so long."

"When was it?"

"It was a few weeks ago. I was on campus to drop off an assignment and let my professor know I skipped class to go to a funeral. I wasn't in much of a mood to talk to anyone."

"I wish I would've seen you. I would've made you talk. The hardest part of not seeing you was not talking to you. I just missed listening to you. It's something about your voice. It's soothing. That and I missed all our crazy conversations. No one else in the world talks about things like you do."

I opened my mouth to respond, but an odd sensation crept from my nose, down my neck, and into my heart. From there, it shot through the rest of my body. The tingling sensation was a mixture of desire and self-restraint, two things that don't belong together. Although we never admitted it to anyone – especially one another – we both still wanted each other, and our location made it worse. She and I always had this thing for couches. In most of the places we both lived, we found a quiet couch away from the rest of the house where we could smoke and spend time together. Those smoking sessions always ended the same way, the two of us half dressed trying to keep quiet. As we sat on her couch, the little bit of devil in her Angel Eyes drew me in and she couldn't help but give in to my gravity. We'd been apart for a long time, but we never got used to the fact that we couldn't fuck whenever we wanted. In the ten seconds or so we moved closer I ran the scene through my head. It began with me pinning her down on the cushions, and it ended with her biting the back of the couch over my shoulder. There were two problems: she had a boyfriend and I didn't want to be the other guy in her life. No matter how much I wanted her I had to control myself.

"We should go eat," I said.

"Yeah, we should," she looked away and set the roach on the edge of her ashtray. There was a long pause before we actually stood to leave. When she disappeared into the bedroom to get her purse, I heard a key in the door.

Jessica's roommate, Claire, jumped when she opened the door and saw me standing next to the couch. "It's been a while," she said as she dropped her backpack and purse in the dining area. Afterward, she turned to face me, leaning back with both her palms flat on the table. She looked at the floor as she spoke. "I never got a chance to thank you the last time I saw you."

"You don't have to."

She lifted her eyes to look in mine. They were glossed over. "I remember the whole night. I remember Jess putting me on the couch at the party. I remember the guy talking to me. I remember you getting there and carrying me out. I even remember Jess helping me into the apartment. I heard you stayed after we left. You really did a number on the guy that gave me that drink."

"He deserved it."

"He was in a wheelchair."

"You can't walk on crutches with a broken collarbone."

"I don't know why you helped me. We never got along, and you didn't have to do that. I don't know how I'll ever repay you."

"I don't need payment." I heard Jessica come out of the bedroom and stop when she saw Claire and me. Although I knew Jessica was behind me, I kept my eyes on Claire. "I got you out of that house because it was the right thing to do. I stayed behind and fought those guys for me."

8

"Guys?" Claire asked, tilting her head and clenching her teeth behind open lips.

Jessica stepped up next to me and cut into the conversation. "Mike fought everyone that lives in that house. He was a mess when I went and picked him up, but he hurt some of those guys pretty bad. One guy's jaw was wired shut."

"He talked too much anyway." I said to lighten the mood.

Jessica shushed me before she continued. "I never told you because we never really talked about what happened."

Claire's eyes filled her face. Although the altercation took place months earlier, the memory of such traumatic events always feel like it happened yesterday. Her gaze returned to the floor before she started speaking again. "I guess I owe you more than I thought."

"You don't owe me anything." I turned to Jess. "You ready to go eat?"

Jessica smiled and nodded and walked toward the door, waving goodbye to her roommate in silence. Claire grabbed my arm before I could walk out. When I turned around, she slipped her arms around my neck, whispering "Thank you" in my ear and kissing me on the cheek, the moisture from her lips a favour for her knight in not so shiny armor.

I was holding the door open for Jessica with one hand, so I returned the hug with my free arm. "Anytime," I said. I was quiet the whole way to the diner.

When we got to the Steak and Egg Diner right off Wisconsin, I parked in front of the dumpster in the small parking lot out back. We rounded the building and the pastel picket fence that surrounded the property. Although it was warm for the beginning of November, it was still too cool for patio seating. When we walked inside there was only one person working behind the diner's empty twelve seat bar, the only seating inside the diner. Steak and Egg was more famous for its breakfast items than its dinner, and it was one of the only places in the area that was open twenty-four hours a day. They did the majority of their business after the bars closed. The diner had a decent morning and lunch crowd, but the place was usually empty at dinner time – Jess' and my favorite time to dine there.

We grabbed our usual seats at the far left by the dishwasher. It had been a while since we'd been in, but the evening cook still remembered us. He grabbed us a couple waters before we were settled in. We both ordered a coffee and we knew what we wanted to eat before we even got there. We ate the same things every time. I got the Old South Sunday, a big breakfast meal with biscuits and gravy, sausage, bacon, two eggs, and hash browns. Jess always ordered two eggs over easy, with hash browns and white toast.

While we waited for our food, we watched the cook do his work in the small, exposed kitchen behind the bar. It was a hell of a show to watch the cook prepare three plates for two people, but it was a mind blowing act when the restaurant was full. When the patio was open, they could have forty or more customers at any given time. Although they had enough wait staff to cover the entire floor with ease, there was only enough room for two cooks to cover the line. Most of the cooks had been with the restaurant for years, and they learned to do a lot with very little space and equipment. They only had one freezer and a three door cooler for food storage. As far as cooking equipment, from left to right the kitchen had an automatic fry machine, a gravy urn, two stove-top burners, a two by four feet flat grill, a four slot toaster, and a waffle iron. To make matters worse, the toaster and waffle iron were in the middle of the expo station (for those unfamiliar with restaurant lingo, expo is where meals are plated for delivery).

When the cook prepared our food he began by getting a couple biscuits out of the freezer and setting them on the flat grill. He set a couple steel rings next to the biscuits, stuffed them full of hash browns, and doused them with vegetable oil so they'd cook a nice, golden brown. Afterward, he set pre-cooked sausage patties and strips of bacon by the biscuits and potatoes. He cracked four eggs into two skillets and set them on the burners. He stepped to the side and started the toast. All at once he flipped the food on the grill with his right hand and flipped the eggs in the skillet with his left. When the hash browns were nearly done he slipped the rings off the potatoes and onto the spatula, hanging the rings on hooks over his head. He set three plates in the small expo space. The biscuits got their own plate and he doused them with a ladle full of gravy on his way to set the plate in front of me. As he walked back toward the empty plates he grabbed both skillets and slid the eggs onto their respective plates. In two trips he plated the hash browns and protein. The toast popped up as if he'd raised it with telekinesis. He

10

buttered and sliced the toast before turning to drop off the last of our food. Jess and I only took our eyes off the show when our food was in front of us and the cook returned to his crossword puzzle.

"Can I have your bacon?" she asked and I nodded in response. That was the extent of our conversation any time we went to Steak and Egg. Jess and I didn't need words to communicate while we ate. We'd eaten together enough the act was second nature. I usually left the plate of biscuits and gravy between Jess and me so she could eat some. She'd usually set a piece of toast on my plate as payment for the bacon I gave her, but she never gave me anything for the biscuit and all the gravy she stole. She said it was 'community food' if I tried to complain.

The cook folded our check lengthwise and slipped it next to my plate without saying anything. I dropped cash with a decent tip right before we walked out the door. I usually left about thirty per cent, which was why the staff remembered Jess and me.

The temperature had dropped and it was starting to feel a lot more like November in the District. "Wanna smoke one more before we call it a night?" I asked as I opened the passenger door for her.

"Sounds good."

Once I was in, I started the truck and backed out of the parking area onto Chesapeake Street. I drove to River Road and turned north. We huddled against the vents for warmth but the engine took as much time to warm up as it took to drive to my place. Jess rubbed her shoulders to make up for the heat that wasn't coming out of the vents and I tried to keep my mind off the cold, thinking warm thoughts as I drove. Once we were moving Jess turned in her seat, scrunching her eyebrows in discomfort. It was too cold to talk, but Jess was going to stare at me until she made me uncomfortable enough to start a conversation.

"You want to ask me something."

"I do." Her face relaxed. "Have you worked on my book at all?"

"I haven't worked on the book since the beginning of summer."

"Why not?"

"It doesn't feel right writing a book for you when we're both seeing other people."

"So don't write it for me."

"I promised you a book a long time ago. Chasing Angels will always be the book I wrote for you. I was writing it in hopes I might get you

11

back when I finished it. When I met Portia, I set it aside and I haven't looked at it since."

"When you made that promise, you told me you were writing because you wanted to conquer the world. You said writing a great book was the greatest challenge you could think of and it was the best way to test whether you really can do anything you set your mind to."

"That was my intention, but the only book I've been able to write is the one I've been writing to get you back. Since we broke up, conquering the world kinda got moved to the back burner."

"How are you going to do it anyway?"

"Do what?"

"Conquer the world."

"An explanation of my life's work would require a lifetime of explanation. But, in short, I'm gonna convince the human race that I'm the most qualified person to lead them. I just have to figure out where to begin. That's been the hardest part. I can't convince anyone of anything if I don't have an audience."

"Maybe you should focus on the book and let the other pieces fall into place. You know, be the bull."

We'd already finished the short drive back to my apartment. We hurried after we got out of the truck, trying to make it to the warmth of my bedroom as fast as we could. Once we were inside I went to work rolling a joint while she snooped around my bookshelves.

"What are you looking for?" I asked.

"I'm just looking. I forgot about all these books." She squatted down behind my chair and reached toward the bottom of the bookshelf. "Look at all these notebooks. Are these all since you started college?"

"Those are the ones that fit inside the notebook sleeve you gave me."

"There are fifteen notebooks here. How many pages is that?"

"Well, some of the notebooks are eighty pages and others are a hundred. That puts the count somewhere between twelve and fifteen hundred…shit, double that because they're either eighty or a hundred sheets, not pages. So that means it's closer to three thousand."

"And it's all by hand, too. How the hell did you find the time to write this much in three and a half years of college?"

"I write in my notebooks instead of paying attention in class. It builds the illusion that I'm a good student."

"But three thousand pages?"

"It's not quite three thousand."

"If I didn't know you so well, I would never believe this was possible. What's it like?"

"What's what like?"

"Being different from everyone else…not being human."

"What makes you think I'm not human?"

"The fact that I know you so well. You're definitely not human. You're whatever comes next."

I turned around and lit the joint. I passed the joint to Jessica, blowing the smoke out and saying, "I guess that makes me one of a kind."

"That's for sure." As she passed the joint back to me, she pulled a notebook off the shelf and took her usual seat at the edge of the bed. She lowered her face and flipped through the notebook as she asked again, "So what's it like?"

"It's scary as all hell." I took a hit. "And infinitely lonely. I've been close to a few people, but I can never really relate to anyone. Sometimes I don't think I ever will, but I didn't mind getting close to you. I don't mind it with Portia. I think I'm finally used to always feeling alone as long as I have someone to talk to every once in a while."

"I'm always here if you need someone to talk to."

"It's not the same. It probably never will be."

"You can't predict the future."

"Sometimes I can."

"You know what I mean." She rolled her eyes and leaned forward on the notebook she was reading.

I rested my elbows on my knees as I matched her gesture. "So do you."

Something in the air was Feelin' Way Too Damn Good. She knew what I was capable of. She'd seen me predict the future and read minds. That was the part of me she fell in love with – like Lois Lane falling for Superman. I figured those feelings were welling up from somewhere deep inside because her body started moving closer. I couldn't help but do the same. We were close enough our legs were mixed together

13

between our seats and that same tingling sensation crept though my whole body again. I gripped the back of her calf and pulled her closer. My heart beat harder. Her cheeks flushed and her eyes closed. I gripped her leg tighter and pulled harder. When our foreheads touched I heard those ill fated words I heard every time she and I tried to Collide.

"I can't."

"Neither can I, but that doesn't change the fact that I really want to."

"So do I, but I'm still in a relationship. I don't want to hurt him like that."

"I don't want to hurt Portia either, but I've wanted this a long time." Our foreheads were still together when we opened our eyes. My hands were shaking. There was no going further, but there was no taking it back. Although nothing ever actually happened between us, I still felt hurt by nothing's proximity. And I knew the situation hurt Jessica no matter how much she tried to hide it.

How could two people who still had such strong feelings for one another be so cruel to themselves? I'd spent so long looking for A Feeling Like That, but I wouldn't just move on. Jessica told me how much she still loved me every day, but she wouldn't let herself just be *in* love with me.

I got up from the chair and walked into the kitchen to smoke. I was half way down the cigarette before she joined me. She'd already donned her coat and she had her purse over her shoulder. "I should probably go."

"I'll drive you."

"I just called a cab."

I looked anywhere but at her. If her eyes caught mine there would be nothing to stop me from running to her, pressing her lips to mine, and fucking her brains out. When I ran out of places to look in the kitchen I searched my pockets. I pulled out my phone to check the time. It was already eight thirty. Portia would be by soon. "If you want me to drive you we have to leave now. If you want to take a cab that's fine, too, but I have plans in half an hour."

"My cab'll be here in twenty minutes or less."

"I'll walk you." I grabbed my jacket and led Jessica toward the door. We both stared at the floor in front of us as we walked down the hall toward the main entrance. "I guess I failed at moving on over the last couple months," I said as we stepped outside.

She scrunched her chin and nodded before she responded. "I didn't do any better. I guess some feelings will never die no matter how much we try and kill them."

We smoked a cigarette outside while we waited together. I didn't know what to say and I didn't think she had any idea either. Only one thing was certain, there was no denying the feelings we still had for one another. It was easy to let those feelings go when we were apart, but proximity set off our weaknesses for one another. Like the force of gravity the force of our attraction varied inversely with the square of the distance between us. Any closer and there wouldn't have been a force in the known universe strong enough to separate us.

"You just make sure that I get my chance when things end between you two," I said as the cab pulled up in front of us. Rain was starting to stain the concrete around us. Jess was going to make it out just before it started to fall.

She stepped to the door, but she turned to answer before she got in. "Don't worry. I'll keep my promise. I always do."

"The offer always stands," I said. She paused and nodded before she got in the cab, leaving me alone in the cold November Rain.

About the time I lost sight of Jessica's cab, Portia texted me to let me know she was on her way. I walked back to my apartment and sanitized the bedroom. What can I say, I get a little paranoid when I'm high and I didn't want Portia to notice the ass print at the edge of the bed. My phone vibrated in my pocket a second time and I took one last look around for any sign that Jessica was just there. I didn't have to read the message to know Portia was on her way to the door. I saw her jogging across the parking lot when I stepped outside. After a quick kiss, we hurried inside to the bedroom.

Once we were in the bedroom, she unbuttoned her jacket slowly, holding her nose in the air. "Are you high?"

"Maybe?"

She hit me on the shoulder as she dropped her jacket to the floor. "Why don't you wait to get high with me? You know I like to smoke a little after I finish teaching yoga." She hit me again.

"Stop it, Jessica."

15

It took me about half a second to realize what I did. I wasn't sure if she heard me, so I tried to play it off like nothing happened. I was a fool to think she didn't notice.

"Make it right." The only part of her that moved was her lips.

"I don't know how." I admitted defeat with my intonation. My voice was as low as the Dead Sea.

"Make it right, Michael."

"What am I supposed to say?"

She finally turned to face me with her hands on her hips. "I'm guessing Jessica is the ex-girlfriend that hurt you so bad. You better live up to your oversized ego right now and say the perfect thing."

"I saw her today. We hadn't talked in months and we had dinner-" I figured telling The Truth was better than nothing, but I still lacked the courage to look at her as I spoke. "She and I stopped talking the night I got into that fight. That night we agreed to see one another today. I forgot about it until she texted me this morning."

"This wouldn't be a big deal if you would have just told me. You could've been up front and honest and this would be just fine. I'm fine with you talking to her as long as you just want to be friends with her."

"I'm not sure what I want anymore."

"That's not what I want to hear from you right now."

"I haven't written since the problems started between me and her. I need to start writing again."

"Do whatever you want." She picked up her jacket and slammed the bedroom door after she walked out. Another moment later I heard the main door slam. I didn't go after her. From that moment forward She Was The One That Got Away and I was okay with it. I figured I'd already lost her to the Words I Couldn't Say so why waste the energy. I sat in my chair with my face in my hands feeling sorry for myself, but I only did that for the space of thirty seconds. There were two things I had to do to make this situation right for all parties involved. The first was letting Portia move on. She was beautiful, inside and out, and I couldn't drag her down. Within two minutes of her storming out I'd already done the best possible thing I could do for her, nothing. The next part was going to take a little more time.

Growing up, every teacher I ever had told me I could do anything to which I set my mind. I figured every kid my age heard that, so I set out to put that theory to the test. When I was ten, I set my mind on conquering the world. I dedicated my whole life to it, and, since then, it has destroyed every relationship I've ever tried to build – family, friends, and girlfriends. I didn't tell anyone my secret for a long time. It was my cross to bear, and I thought anyone I told would think I was crazy. Jessica was the first person I told about it. I told her I wanted to write a book to prove I had what it took to conquer the world, but the only book I wrote was the one I wrote for her. When Portia walked out the door I realized <u>Chasing Angels</u> was the book I needed. Jessica was right. I had to finish her book and let the other pieces fall into place. The book was a perfect way to build an audience. It was the perfect way to convince the world I was the man to lead them. I wanted to run the world, so why not write a resumé for the position. It was the starting point I spent so long looking for. Although I could've spent the rest of my life happy with Portia, I had to stay the course. I had to finish Jessica's book.

Once the manuscript was out of my file cabinet's bottom drawer I looked at my computer, searching for the file on my desktop. Although I tried to forget about the novel while I was with Portia, I remembered every detail of what I'd written before I gave up in June. When I put my hands to the keyboard, the motions of my fingers felt natural, like I never stopped working on it at all. Even though I didn't consider scribbling in a notebook real writing, those scribbles kept me in practice.

When I stopped working on the novel, I forgot about Jessica and fell in love with Portia. Forgetting is not the same as moving on, and my love for Jessica would always outweigh any other love as long as that novel remained unfinished. Even if I changed everything I'd written to revolve around Portia, Jessica was the genesis of the idea, and there was no way I could ever alter the idea's conclusion. That would destroy the whole connection between Sera, the title, and the last page. The story was all about chasing the last page.

Chapter 6

"You stare at that phone any harder it might fall in love with you."
Mike lit the joint as Holt slipped the phone back in his pocket. The
walk-in refrigerator was cold, but it was the best place to smoke in the
daylight. The ventilation changed the air in the space every couple
minutes, and the low temperature made it impossible to smell anything.
"You probably won't even get a signal in here."

"I'm supposed to meet Sera in a little bit." Holt hit the joint and
punched Mike. "And fuck you for telling her I'm in town."

"Hey, I didn't tell her."

"Don't lie to me." Holt drew his arm back like he was about to
backhand Mike.

"I'm not lying. I told Caitlin and she mentioned it to Sera. They
share everything, you know."

"You don't have to share everything with Cait."

"I hadn't planned on it. Cait knew something was up when she met
Sera here last night and I was drunk at work. She pulled me back into
the office and beat it out of me."

"I thought you were some big, bad, Navy man. You're letting some
woman beat information out of you?"

"We may be married, but that won't stop Cait from cuttin' my
thumbs off when she's mad."

"Now you see why I'm so nervous about seeing Sera." Holt
scrambled for his phone when it vibrated in his pocket. He stared at the
screen and breathed a sigh of relief.

"Sera?" Mike asked.

"Alex. Hold on a sec," Holt answered the phone. "Hey, what's going
on?"

"Just checking in on you and seeing if you wanted to grab an early
lunch."

"I'm actually in New Jersey right now. I'm supposed to meet with
Sera in a little bit to…sign everything."

"Oh. I should let you go then. I'm sorry if I'm interrupting
anything."

"You're not interrupting. I'm just smoking weed in a big
refrigerator. How was yesterday?"

"That sounds…weird. Anyway, yesterday was pretty quiet. I spent most of the day on the phone with the clients we're losing and I spent a lot of time reading over some of the new submissions. I've got some stuff to show you whenever you get back to New York. We've got a couple really promising manuscripts in the last couple weeks. You'd know that if you ever did any work while you were at work."

"That's what I have you for."

"When are you meeting with Sera?"

"Whenever she calls. I'll let you know how everything goes."

"Okay. I'm just hanging around the house today. My phone's on if you need anything."

"Thanks, talk to you soon."

Mike's eyes were locked on Holt when he ended the call. Mike had one eyebrow raised and his head was leaned forward. "Isn't Alex your assistant?"

"Yes, and she's one of my only friends in New York. We've worked together a long time."

"How long have you two been seeing each other?"

"What makes you think Alex and I are seeing each other?"

"The fact that I'm not stupid. I thought you said you never cheated on Sera."

"I didn't. She and I didn't start sleeping together until after Sera left. It's nothing serious, just fun."

"Yet she calls you at nine on a Saturday morning to check on you and ask you to lunch. Sounds a little more than casual."

"We're good friends that just happen to sleep together every once in a while."

"When was the last time?"

"Night before last."

"But it's not serious." Mike passed Holt the joint and walked to the exit. "Finish that. I'll be right back."

Holt pulled on the joint and stared at his phone looking for the text Sera had not yet sent. Other than Holt's occasional cough, the only sound in the walk-in was the hum of the ventilation fan and the refrigerant compressor. He shook his head when he realized his high was really setting in. This was the first time he smoked for real in a couple years, and it was really getting to him. He smiled for no reason as the joint fizzled out. When Mike came back in the room Holt was trying to solve a Sudoku on his phone.

"Are you really standing in the walk-in playing games on your phone?" Mike asked as he walked back in the door.

"I was waiting for you."

"You could have waited outside in the un-refrigerated space." Mike motioned for Holt to follow him into the kitchen. "I'm gonna have to get to work. The kitchen guys are gonna show up soon, and I gotta get 'em rollin'. You gonna make it through this meeting with Sera?"

"I'll be fine."

"She's gonna be pissed that you're showing up high."

"She won't even notice."

"Fat chance." Mike started to walk toward the front of the bar, but he stopped short. "I almost forgot. I picked up last night after I got off work. Here's your half. Do you even have anything to smoke out of?"

Holt stuffed the bag of weed in his pocket with his cigarettes and phone in hopes the over filled pocket would keep a police officer from finding it. "I still have your papers. How much do I owe you?"

"Call it an early birthday present."

"My birthday was four months ago."

"Then call it a late one. Just don't leave town without saying goodbye."

"I'll get a hold of you later, brother." Holt walked out the back exit into the alley behind the bar. The sun was still low over the ocean, and the ocean was on the other side of the building. When he passed a dumpster he slowed down to check the shadows on the far side. When he came to the street at the end of the alley he moved slowly around the corner to check for any bystanders on the sidewalk. He walked in the side entrance of his hotel and went up the back stairs, avoiding the front desk and the complimentary continental breakfast goers.

He waited for Sera on his balcony and watched the waves against the shore. He lit a cigarette, dragging so hard he could hear the tobacco crackle as it burned. The thought of Sera showing up with a gun to kill him came to mind, and he pondered the odds that his vision was correct. She sounded happy to see him when they spoke on the phone the night before, but she sounded upset with the idea when he heard her at the sea wall moments later. There was no telling which way the next hour would go, but Holt was ready to get it over with. He would leave New Jersey. She could have it. Sure, it meant that he may not see Mike very often and he may never see the twins again, but he wasn't about to wind up a part of Sera's life anytime soon. Not after she left the way she did. Not after she sent divorce papers.

When the text message finally came, he was halfway through his third cigarette. She said that she was leaving her dad's house in the message, and it was only a five minute drive to the hotel. Even if she walked it would only take her ten minutes. Holt pulled the cherry out of the cigarette and walked to the front of the hotel to meet her. He relit the cigarette outside and waited until he saw Sera make her way around the corner onto Ocean Avenue. After she came into view he flicked the cigarette into the gutter and walked to her.

"Hey, pretty lady," Holt said, giving her a quick hug and a kiss on the cheek. "How've you been?"

"Alive I guess." She returned the kiss on the cheek as she pulled away. When she stepped back she was only a half pace in front of Holt, and both her hands gripped the straps of the purse over her shoulder. She squinted her sunward eye as she asked, "When did you start smoking again? I haven't seen you smoke a cigarette in years."

"About an hour after I realized you left that night. I cracked a bottle of bourbon, so a pack of cigarettes only seemed natural."

"I guess that makes sense. Can we go inside and talk?"

Holt motioned Sera toward the hotel entrance. As he turned to follow he said, "I'm on the top floor across from the stairs."

When they started going up the stairs, Holt realized he should have led the way to the room. As he followed, her waist lined up directly with his eyes. Her ass was his second favorite part of her body, and it was exceptional. She knew how to wear a pair of jeans. They fit well, but they were loose enough around the waist to avoid a muffin top. That was one of Holt's pet peeves. He hated back fat. He didn't like a bony woman, but he loved when women knew how to dress themselves. And Sera dressed that ass well. Although it was right in front of him, he held out until the third and final flight of stairs before he gave her back pockets a long look. He felt bad for looking because he found other great asses since she left, but the view brought back a string of memories and emotions that mesmerized him.

21

When they got to the top of the stairs Sera stepped to the side and looked at Holt. His eyes went straight from her ass to his favorite part of her body, but her shoulders were covered by the old t-shirt she was wearing.

"Are you gonna open the door?" she asked with an inquisitive smile.

He shook his head and looked back at her head, reaching in his pocket for his key. "I was just getting ready to do that."

Sera leaned in, squinting as she examined his face. Her smile faded. "No, you weren't. You're high. You forgot the door was locked."

Holt tried to smile as he held the door open for her. "I didn't forget because I'm high. I-"

"So you admit it? You're high." She dropped her bag by the door and walked halfway across the room. When she stopped and turned she locked her right hip, pointing her left foot at Holt and crossing her arms. "The first time we see each other in five months and you show up stoned."

"In all fairness I came to New Jersey to see Mike. He and I made plans to smoke this morning long before you called me last night. Consider yourself lucky I picked up at all."

Sera's head moved back as the words hit her. Her arms relaxed, but they didn't uncross all the way. They fell so she was holding each wrist with the opposite hand. She walked the rest of the way toward the bed and took a seat, sitting on her hands. "I'm sorry. It's been too long. I'm just a little emotional considering everything that's happened in the last few months."

"Me, too."

"How've you been?" she asked.

"I've been drinking too much and slipping at work. Alex has pretty much been carrying my career since you left. I was trying to buy a place at the Dakota, but I'm not sure if I can afford it anymore. It's too big to live in alone anyway."

"I'm sure you'd never spend a night alone there. You could find some company in New York."

"I'm not in the business of going home with every girl I meet anymore. Last time I checked I graduated from college a decade ago."

"And you've been married ever since."

"Married to you. And you left me on our anniversary. I had two great gifts for you that night. That was when I started looking at the apartment in the Dakota. I wanted to surprise you with that and then give you the other one."

"What was the other gift?"

"I wrote something for you."

"I don't want to talk about your writing. I think you know why."

"Will you just hear me out?" Holt walked over to the backpack by the desk. He pulled out his manuscript of <u>Failing Aristotle</u> and handed it to Sera. "I rewrote this right before you left. I was gonna give it to you after I told you about the place at the Dakota. I want you to have it."

"This isn't my book…not all of it at least."

"It's my half. It may not be the exact same one I wrote back in college, but it's the same story. This one's better."

"I thought Cait and I had the only copies." With every word her head moved farther forward and her eyes narrowed a little more.

"So you do have it?" He sat up and pointed his chin at her, happy she volunteered information he was sure he would have to drag out of her. "When did you take it?"

"Stop trying to read my mind." She reached inside her bag and pulled out the envelope, setting it on the bed next to her and nodding toward it as she spoke. "I took it the day I took the backpack. I'm surprised it took you this long to figure it out. I brought it down here to show it to Mike."

"Mike doesn't need to know."

"He's your best friend – or at least he used to be. He has a right to know you've been lying to him all this time. You owe him that after everything he's done for you. How do you think he would feel if he saw this," she said as she raised <u>Failing Aristotle</u> with both hands, waving the manuscript back and forth in front of her face.

"Mike's a trusting guy. I'd tell him the truth: that I rewrote it from memory."

"Mike's trusting because he's honest. He never would have done this to you."

"No, he wouldn't have. But it's my mistake – my secret. That book came around before I met you. When I wrote about you, you were just a girl I stared at around campus. It may have been the deciding factor for you running away to Denver with a guy you barely knew, but the envelope is between Mike and me."

"And Cait. What do you think she'd do if she found out?"

"Cait would maim me and force me to live without arms, legs, or a dick. At least Mike would just kill me."

"So you're scared to let them know. I guess I know what that cross on your back is all about."

"I told you about that cross a long time ago. It's not just about what's in the envelope."

"You told me, but you could have lied about that plan, too."

"I never lied about our plan. We just failed."

"You, plural, did not fail, Holt. Mike kept up his end of the deal. He built his bar from the ground up. You singularly failed for the both of you. You're the one that didn't mail the envelope. Don't you dare drag Mike in on your failure. He's a good man. *You* let him down when you stopped writing to be an agent."

"I tried to start writing again when I wrote that." Holt pointed across the room at the manuscript. "Will you at least take it and read it? Maybe let me know what you think."

"I'll take it, but I'm not going to read it."

"You scared you'll fall in love with me all over again?"

"What makes you think I ever stopped loving you? I never would have expected you to be so naïve. I'm still madly in love with you. A while back I went home so we could work everything out, but you were occupied. So I left again, and I took your bag and our wedding rings and the picture and the envelope with me. And there's not a chance in hell that I'm going to read your new book until you come clean about your old one," she said as she rested her hand on the envelope at her side.

Holt gripped his chin with his thumb and index finger, shaking his head and looking at the floor as he spoke. "I'm sorry, but I can't do that."

"Then the only choice we're left with is divorce."

"I guess that's fair." Holt turned the desk chair around and stuffed his arm back inside the backpack. When he pulled his arm out, he had both the tri-folded affidavits in his hand. He opened them to make sure he had the divorce papers. At the top of the desk there was a hotel pen placed neatly on the stationary. "I just sign where the pages are marked, right?"

"Stop being so dramatic. I didn't mean it like that."

"What other way is there to mean it? It looks like the red tabs are mine and the yellow is you. I'll be done in a minute." He signed the first respondent line so hard the final swoop of the pen dragged clear to the edge of the page. He flipped to the next marked page without reading. Before he could sign, a soft hand gripped his, preventing the next signature. He turned to face his wife. "I thought this is what you wanted."

"I never wanted to divorce you, but Matt asked me to move to Florida with him. I haven't said 'yes' yet, but I don't want to move there with him if I'm still married to you."

"Wow. You move fast. You tell him you love him already, too?" He turned the chair to face her.

"Yes." The short pause between her statements gave Holt a momentary glance inside her mind. The silence was enough to show she honestly loved Matt, but it was conditional. "I do love him."

"Last time I checked we dated for almost nine months before you said that to me. You haven't been in New Jersey that long."

"He and I dated for two and a half years before I met you. All those old feelings came rushing back when he and I started dating again."

"Or you're just telling him you love him so you don't have to mean it with me."

She turned back to the bed. "Get out of my head. I've felt you tooling around in there since I brought up the envelope." When she sat back down, she looked anywhere but the direction of Holt's eyes. She knew that was the only way to hide from his superpower.

"How long have you been dating him?" he asked, leaning forward and looking at the floor. She was well on the defensive so he decided to give her a break.

"About as long as you've been fucking the girl with auburn hair." she said as she looked back at Holt, taking every advantage of his mercy. "What is that, about four months now?"

Holt curled his toes inside his shoes as Brandi's face flashed in his mind. Luckily he had the presence of mind to move the involuntary response somewhere it went unnoticed. "How do you know about that?"

25

"Don't ask how I know. Just know that I know."

Holt looked back to the floor, pressing his hands together like he was about to pray for forgiveness, but he didn't pray. He rubbed his hands back and forth trying to see between them as he spoke. "That's as over as you and me now. I'm sure you don't care, but that's the truth."

"You're right. I don't care." Sera stood up and crossed her arms as she turned toward the back of the room. Her bottom lip was tucked behind her teeth as she turned to shut the door. Maybe a little time out was what they both needed.

Holt pulled out a cigarette as he walked toward the balcony door. He heard the bathroom sink turn on as he stepped outside. He leaned on the rail and stared at the beach. It was almost ten o'clock. Umbrellas were going up, chez lounge chairs were opening, and towels were going down. The tide was already gone, so the surfers were no longer waiting out past the second break hoping for a good wave. Most were probably back in their surf shacks getting high. That sounded like a good way to deal with the stress brought on by the meeting with Sera, but Holt would have to figure that out after she left. He just sucked down the cigarette and hoped the mild oxygen deprivation would slow his enraged heart rate.

When he went back inside, Sera was still in the bathroom. The water was still running, but he never heard the toilet flush. He knew why she was in there, but there was nothing he could do about it. At the desk he unfolded both of the legal documents he had to sign. He read nothing. Instead, he focused on the jarring reality between the lines of the papers. Not only would he be homeless in another six days, he would be single as well. He spent the last few months hiding from impending change. Now, he had to start dealing with it. It was probably a good idea to reserve a hotel for Friday night. There was no staying in the apartment next weekend. Alex would take him in, but that would be wildly inappropriate. For someone as put together as Holt, he needed to handle his business.

Sera wiped the corners of her nose with toilet tissue as she walked out of the bathroom. Outside the door, she paused to finish and set the soiled paper on top of the dresser. She remained still as she stood by the bathroom door. Her eyes were even. Her lips were flat. Her eyebrows were neutral. Her spine and head were plumb.

Holt's feet were so far apart his knees turned in under the weight of his elbows. His back was hunched so his head could rest in his hands. His right hand gripped the hair on the top of his head while his left hand rubbed the stubble on the side of his jaw. It was uncomfortable as hell, but it felt better than another awkward conversation with the woman he was about to divorce. Neither moved until Sera broke the silence.

"I'm sorry I left," she said as she relaxed her rigid form.

"I'm sorry I never came after you," he said as he straightened himself out.

"Can we put off signing everything for a day or two? I can't handle it right now."

"I'm okay with that. Maybe we can try and be friends while I'm around. I spent a good portion of my life with you." Holt looked at the floor again. "I guess I miss you a little."

"I miss you, too. I'll admit it." She tipped her head back and looked at the ceiling. Maybe gravity would keep the tears inside. "My dad's having a bar-be-que tomorrow if you want to come. I'm sure he'd like to see you before you leave."

"I'll be there."

"You can bring a date."

"Mike's the only date I'm gonna bring. I wouldn't do that to you."

"Matt's gonna be there."

"I'll be fine." He set his hands on the papers. "We'll table this for now."

"I can live with that." She smiled and walked toward the bed. It looked like she was about sit back down but she stopped short of her previous seat, kneeling with her back to Holt. He leaned to the side trying to look over her shoulder, but her purse zipped shut before he had a chance to see what she had done. In an instant her bag was over her shoulder and she was walking toward the door.

"Leaving already?" Holt asked as he snapped to his feet. His eyes remained locked on her as he followed her across the room.

"I've just really missed you and I'm getting emotional and I need some fresh air." She turned toward him holding her bag with both hands as it hung between her feet. "I'll see you tomorrow."

"Most definitely." He wrapped his arms around her and her bag hit his calves as she did the same. They stood like that for a minute, squeezing tighter and adjusting their heads to get closer than they had been for five months. When they started to let go their faces paused inches apart. They looked one another over from lips to foreheads. Their arms slid down one another until they were holding each other by the elbows.

"I guess I'll see you tomorrow," he said. His focus went back and forth between her eyes.

"Yeah." Her eyes tried to keep up with his. For a moment, nothing began again, but neither took it any further. Sera walked out the door and Holt let it fall shut. He put his hands in his pockets and let himself fall forward until his head hit the door. He stood like that with his eyes closed until his hand came across a plastic baggy he forgot about.

When he turned around, Holt realized what Sera had done just before she left. Her abrupt departure interrupted his curiosity, but her absence gave him a chance to update his situational awareness. The envelope was still sitting on the edge of the bed, but, other than that, the bed was empty. He took a couple slow steps forward, taking a closer look to make sure his eyes did not deceive him. At first, he was sure Sera had moved or hidden the manuscript he gave her when she first arrived, but further examination showed that was not the case. The manuscript was nowhere to be seen. When he realized Sera must have taken the manuscript, he smiled the kind of smile men rarely smile, wide-eyed with an open mouth and teeth in full view. No matter how minor the gesture, it was more of an olive branch than he ever expected.

Although the thought of <u>Failing Aristotle</u> in Sera's purse put Holt on cloud nine, he sobered up when his attention drifted back toward what she left behind. He went to the bed and picked up the envelope. As he walked toward the desk and sat down, he gave it a quick once-over to make sure no one tampered with it. There was no evidence Sera ever tried to open it, and, other than the normal wear and tear brought on by its age, the envelope was still in great shape. Once Holt was sure his secrets were still well secured, he slipped the envelope inside his backpack and zipped it shut. Concealing the envelope in the bag was not enough to protect his mind, but at least the envelope could only haunt him from there. In an attempt to put his mind elsewhere, he pushed his bag as far underneath the desk and out of sight as possible. Finally, he felt momentarily secure from his demons, a level of content that evaded

28

him since before there ever was an envelope. He knew he would never be at peace as long as the envelope existed, but he was comfortable enough to concentrate on rolling a joint the right way. This time, it only took him one paper and two tries – maybe rolling a j was more like riding a bike than he originally thought.

He was staying in a non-smoking room, and smoking weed on the balcony in the middle of the day was obviously a bad idea. The car would be best. He could just do his old loop through the state park and cut back on the interstate. There was just enough rural area for a joint-long drive. When he was on the road he ordered the Mercedes to call Alex. As the phone rang, he lit up and cracked the window.

"Hey, did you meet with Sera?" she asked when she answered.

"Yeah, she left about twenty minutes ago. I'm going for a drive to clear my head."

"Did you sign everything?"

"No, we just talked. Things got a little heated so we decided to put off the signatures for a day or two."

"Oh, when are you coming home?"

"I'll probably come back on Monday. I'll get a hold of Connor and let him know. He told me to take as much time as I needed to sort everything out, so I may take advantage of that for a couple days."

"Hmmm." There was a long pause on the other end. "I'm not going to say it."

"Don't worry. I'll say it for you. You were right. This is going to be a lot harder than I thought it would be."

"You're not even going to let me say 'I told you so?'"

"Go ahead."

"I told you so."

"Feel better?"

"Much. Talk to you soon?"

"You know it."

Holt ended the call before he got to the interstate. At higher speeds he would be unable to hear Alex over the wind blowing in the window. He was half finished with smoking, and the car was getting a little hazy. After he merged onto the highway he rolled the window down a little more to let the car air out. Before he got off the freeway he ditched the joint and smoked a cigarette while he finished the drive.

When he got back to the hotel, he left his phone in the car and walked across the street to the beach. He had neither a beach pass nor the appropriate attire to go out onto the sand. Instead, he took a seat on a boardwalk bench to watch the waves and the sea of people accumulating on the shore. It was the best way to enjoy his high without thoughts of Sera dragging down a good time. He could have gone to the bar to hang out – Happy Hour would be open in a few minutes – but he was content alone with his thoughts in the crowd.

Cocaine

If you wanna hang out, you've gotta take her out. Cocaine, she don't lie, and that's more than I can say about most people. It's more than just a hell of a drug. It's an honest relief in any situation. It won't make anything better in the long run, but it'll damn sure help you escape your problems temporarily – sometimes that's all it takes to survive the night. Aside from smoking too much weed, I've never been a huge druggie. But I've always reserved cocaine for special occasions ranging from the saddest of sad nights to the happiest of the happy ones. Cocaine was an obvious addition to any good time, but few people have ever taken the time to understand its ability to help out during the bad ones.

The last time I did cocaine was near the end of a long week. It was mid-terms during the fall semester of my senior year. Although the rest of the student body got the weekend off for fall break, the few students that worked full time jobs didn't get the luxury. All a three day weekend meant to me in the middle of October was an extra shift Friday afternoon. I only had a couple classes on Wednesday and Thursday, but I was working a double Friday, Saturday, and Sunday. Although I usually made about a grand in cash on a weekend like that, it meant that I'd be half dead by Monday. Then on Monday I'd start all over again with three classes and a night shift at the bar. That was how college went for me. I hadn't had a full day off in more than two months, and my next day off was nowhere in sight. Whenever I got to the point I felt like I was too exhausted I dug a little deeper until I thought I couldn't dig no more – that's The Only Way I Know.

When I got home from school on Wednesday I came in off the street. Since I was close to the building's office, I made the stop to check my mail. In my experience people get the highest quantity of the worst news by mail, so I never checked my mail more than once a week. My mailbox was always packed to the brim when I finally got around to checking it and that afternoon wasn't any different. There was a lot of crap, so I sorted through everything by the recycling bin in the corner of the room. If it wasn't from someone I knew or a bill, it got round filed. For once in my life I checked my mail and didn't have any bills, but there was an item in the box that caught me off guard. It was a letter

31

from my brother. I hadn't talked to Holt in a long time, and the letter made me nervous.

When I got back to my apartment I took the letter into the bedroom and sat at the computer desk. I pulled open the top drawer of my file cabinet where I kept my drug paraphernalia. I only had a little bit of weed left – not enough to smoke a joint – so I had to get a hold of Gerud Cruso, my dealer. He was a chef I used to work with, and he usually sold most of his weed in the alley behind his restaurant. He wasn't a criminal mastermind or anything. His stash consisted of whatever he picked up that week and his client list was a bunch of people he used to work with. It was easiest to meet with him while he was working, but it meant waiting until after the dinner rush before I could smoke a whole joint.

After I texted Gerud, I loaded the bowl and took as big of a hit as my lungs would allow, holding the smoke in until my chest hurt. By the time I blew out the smoke my head was already lighter, so I opened the letter to find out what my brother had to say.

Dear Mike,

I know we haven't talked in a while, but I felt like I should let you know Sandy died Wednesday October fifth. I don't know if you remember that cough she had when you were back here, but it turned out to be a lot more than we expected. She went back to the doctor a couple days after you left and they diagnosed her with stage III lung cancer. I guess that's what she gets for smoking two packs a day for the last forty years.

The doctors started her on radiation and chemotherapy right away, but there was a problem a couple weeks ago. When she went in for her radiation treatment, she was radiated too long. She received third degree burns along the inside of her esophagus. No matter what the doctors tried, they couldn't get food or water down her throat. After about a week, she finally passed away.

I tried calling, but the number I had for you was disconnected. I don't even know if the address I have is any good. I don't think it matters though. By the time you get this letter, we'll have already buried her. I'm sorry that you had to find out like this.

If you need anything or you just want to talk, give me a call. I'm here for you and all the animals miss the hell out of you. I understand that you're still trying to figure everything out for yourself, but I still love you, little brother. Hopefully you find whatever it is you're looking for. You seemed a little beat up the last time I saw you, but I don't want you to let the world get you down. Life goes on as long as you'll let it.

Your big brother,
Holt

When I was finished reading I refolded the letter and put it back inside the envelope. I stood up and grabbed a special book off the top shelf of the bookshelf on my right. There were memories stashed throughout the books on those shelves, so many I couldn't hope to find them all if I tried. But one book in particular contained the memories I held most dear. I reviewed the items between the pages one by one, but I wasn't examining them in detail. Instead, I took stock and introduced the old memories to the new one that was about to join them. As the ceremony came to a close, I stuffed my brother's envelope between two random pages and slipped the book back on the shelf.

I sat back down and did my best to picture Sandy's face. It was hard to remember what she looked like. I'd only seen her once since I left Kansas to join the Navy. That was when I went home over Spring Break back in March, almost six months ago. My brother was right to assume that I wasn't ready to bring home back into my life on any kind of regular basis, but it was still good of him to let me know about my aunt.

The sound of my phone vibrating on the desk made me jump. I'd been in a daze for twenty minutes by the time I heard back from Gerud. He was at work and he needed a few hours before he could take the time to run outside and meet me. To pass the time I walked across the street to the liquor store. I made the house rule that I didn't drink at home alone anymore, but I could make an exception for a day like today. I had just lost someone close to me and I felt like feeling sorry for myself. I'd like to say that I felt sorry for Sandy, but I already knew that was a waste of time. I wasn't devastated by Sandy's death. Overall I felt numb, and that made me uncomfortable. I just wanted to pretend like I felt something.

I bought a bottle of Jim Beam and left it on the coffee table when I got back to the apartment. I didn't want to be stumbling drunk by the time I went to meet Gerud, so I went back into the bedroom to smoke a little more while I waited. I had another text from him when I sat back down at the desk. "Did anyone tell you about Jim?"

"The server from your restaurant?" I responded. When I worked with Gerud, there was a server there named James, but everyone called him Jim. Jim and I looked almost exactly alike. We were the same height and we had similar builds. Our hair was the same color and both our jaws were narrower than our foreheads. Neither of us shaved all the way. We just trimmed our stubble to keep it short. Like me, Jim was a great employee, if you could get him to wake up in time for work. I sent another text as a joke. "Did he finally get himself fired?"

"No. He died on Monday." Gerud was a smartass, but he wouldn't joke about that. I stared at the message until another popped up beneath it. "I'll fill you in when you get here."

"Can I add a little extra party to my order?"

"White party?"

"Yes, sir."

"I'll see you at nine."

"Nine it is."

My stomach felt like I just drank too much milk, but the feeling didn't stay there long. The heavy feeling left my stomach and drove toward my feet and my fingers. Once the feeling hit the fringes of my digits it went straight to my head. These psychic feelings were usually brought on by a sequence of related events, like figuring out the end of a movie before I watched it. But, other than the fact they were both dead, Sandy and Jim were in no way related.

I shook off the tingling sensation and took a hit. These sensations were driven by some calculation in my subconscious, and I had no real control over it. This time, however, the image in my mind made absolutely no sense. The picture of a Chinook popped in my head and I couldn't shake the thought. Why would the death of two people who lived half a nation away from one another make me think of an Army helicopter? The only possible explanation was a helicopter crash in Afghanistan a month earlier. Nineteen US Navy Seals and two members of the Afghan Army were on board the CH-47 when it went down. I'd heard the highlights of the story on the radio, but I never followed up on it. When I heard the story I had this gut feeling that my old Navy buddy, Jason, was on board, but I never took the time to check.

I had to know. I pulled up a search engine on my computer and typed in 'Afghanistan helicopter crash list of names'. I didn't have to look very hard. There were hundreds of results. It was a big story when it hit the news. American losses overseas had taken a nose dive by that point. The President said he was ending the war and that's what the death tolls were starting to show. But somehow, while this war was ending, I lost another friend. His name was third on the list of casualties. 'Chief Petty Officer Jason R. Workman was survived by his wife and one-year-old son.' We hadn't spoken in years – not since I was stationed in San Diego at the beginning of my enlistment. I didn't even know he was married let alone that he had a kid. Jason wasn't the first friend I lost to the war, but he was the first one I had to find out about from the news.

I read a little further. The helicopter was shot down and crashed in the mountains, pretty typical for the Pashtun region. Worst part of the whole thing was the bird was most likely shot down by an American-made Stinger missile. We gave the Taliban hundreds of them in the early eighties so they could fight off the invading Soviet Union (if you don't believe me watch the movies Rambo III and Charlie Wilson's War). When we invaded after 9/11, they did exactly what we taught them to do twenty years earlier: use the most effective shoulder-fired, anti-aircraft missile ever built to shoot down every helicopter that came within three miles. If I ever got the chance to meet the guy that took the shot, I wouldn't speak to him with anger. I'd tell him I forgave him and I'd beg for his forgiveness. In the end, we were all just soldiers that did our job to the best of our ability. We lost friends on both sides.

I didn't really hurt after getting all that bad news, but, instead, I wanted to hurt. I had a tough time with some shit growing up, and it made me numb. I didn't come from a bad home, but I had really bad luck. A lifetime of bad news gave me the ability to compartmentalize with the best of them. Being with Jessica changed all that. She convinced me that emotions were okay, and I'd done a really good job of allowing a little in when I met her. When everything ended between the two of us, all that emotion was squeezed out. I locked myself down once again. Any normal person would have called their girlfriend after losing three friends, but I ignored mine that first night. I was numb when I heard about Sandy, but I needed to feel something by the time I heard about Jim and Jason. Sure, they all died over the course of the last month, but I found out over the course of an hour.

The bedroom walls felt a little closer than usual, so I decided to take a break from hiding. I picked up the bottle of bourbon as I passed by the coffee table and walked outside. When I got to the flower bed by the loading dock, I cracked the seal, making sure to keep the bottle covered with the brown bag. I spilled the bottle three times in the dirt and took a long drink after the final splash. By this point of my life, I knew well the procedure to say Goodbye To My Homies, but I had to wait until after I saw Gerud before I could do it right.

I smoked a cigarette, holding the bagged bottle between my feet and staring at my phone. I watched the time, hoping the exposure to the nicotine and the cool, autumn air would keep the walls from crashing in on me when I went inside. But watching the clock wouldn't make nine o'clock come any faster. Back in the bedroom, I set the bottle of bourbon on my file cabinet and split what weed I had left into three bowl-sized piles. I figured rationing the weed I had left would help me space out smoking until I could go meet Gerud, but, in the end, it didn't matter. I spent all my time focused on avoiding clocks. Instead of looking at my phone or my computer, I stared at the bottle of bourbon. I wanted to attack it so bad, but I knew marijuana and cocaine would make the booze that much better. Although the news was really starting to eat at me, I didn't shed a tear. I didn't do anything. I didn't reload my pipe. I didn't look away from the liquor bottle. By the time the ringer on my phone dragged me back to reality, there were still three small piles of marijuana on the desk in front of me. I'd done nothing for almost three hours.

Gerud let me know we could meet up a half an hour earlier than expected. He wanted me to come by at eight thirty so he could get started with his paperwork and finish at a decent hour. To say I was relieved would be a vast understatement. I was pretty sure the only people that stare at one point in a room for three hours without blinking were psychopaths and people about to commit suicide. I had no idea which group I was closest to. I practically ran to my truck. It only took me five minutes to get to Tenleytown, but I parked on River Road and walked the rest of the way. Before I got to Wisconsin Avenue, I cut down an alley that passed behind the restaurant. Gerud came out the back door a few minutes after I texted him that I was outside.

"It's been a long time since you've partied like this. You usually don't get any blow."

"It's a special occasion." I lit a cigarette and offered the pack to Gerud. The drug money was flush up against the pack. He slipped the cash in his pocket as he pulled out a cigarette. When he handed the pack back to me, there was a baggie with it. I'd worked with Gerud in the past and I'd been buying from him for a couple years. I never asked to see him weigh the stash and he never counted the money I handed him. I liked to think we were at least on the border of friendship and the business relationship was out of necessity for both of us.

After we both lit up I continued our conversation. "The last time I saw Jim was the last time I did coke. We were both shitfaced doing lines off the toilet seats next door. He knew I was driving that night and he made me do it to sober up."

"Yeah I'm sure he really twisted your arm."

"That's Jim for you – was Jim. How'd you hear?"

"We found out at work yesterday. Marcus wasn't scheduled, but he showed up for the lunch shift. Black as he is he was so pale you could see right through him. He said he saw online that Jim passed away and he figured we probably needed someone to cover the shift. Didn't say another word the rest of the day."

"He always had a thing for Jim." Marcus was gay and his ultimate fantasy was a foursome with me, Jim, and another server named Luciano. All three of us were tall, dark, ruggedly handsome, and we looked eerily similar. Plus, all three of us were almost the exact same age. We were probably as close as Marcus would ever come to three sexy, male triplets. The news reduced his fantasy to twins. "I'm sure he's taking it pretty hard, harder than he should."

"We all are. I closed up last night and I had to delete him from the computer. I deleted him. It was so...final."

"I'm sorry you had to do that, man. That doesn't sound easy."

"It wasn't, but someone had to do it."

"Have you heard when the funeral is?"

"There's a service tomorrow at eleven. It's at Westmoreland Baptist Church. You know where that is?"

"It's right down the street from my place. You goin'?"

"I'll be there. The owner and his brother are coming in tomorrow to cover for management and we're gonna have all the new guys here to cover the shift. That way all the people that worked with Jim so long can go to the service."

"That's good. Tell everyone I'll see 'em tomorrow. I just wish it was for a better reason."

"Will do. You enjoy that."

We dropped our cigarettes and went our own ways, him back to work and me back to my truck. I didn't go straight home. I couldn't. Instead, I wandered around the back roads chain smoking cigarettes and listening to music. Secretly I prayed to hear this song or that, but the music never matched my mood. I would have loved to hear sad song after sad song, but the world was more inclined to hear the happy-go-lucky ones. I made it all over my part of town that night, circling through the residential areas around The University and up the back roads into Bethesda. There's a little park that surrounds the public pool on the south side of Bethesda. I pulled onto one of the side streets that didn't have any houses or condos.

The vial of cocaine was in the same sack as the weed. When I opened the baggy the smell of marijuana filled the truck. It probably would have been a better idea to just go home and do this, but I wasn't ready to lock myself up for the night. Portia was already texting to see what I was doing, but I didn't know what to say to her. I just wanted to get fucked up and be alone. I poured a little powder on the back of my hand where my thumb came together with my palm. I was careful to keep my thumb pulled in tight enough not to leave an opening, but not so tight that my hand started shaking. When I opened the plastic vial, I kept the lid nearly closed. That way the only thing that fell onto my hand was loose powder and all of the rocks stayed inside. When I had a little pile on the back of my hand, I lifted it toward my face. I paused taking some time to look before I leapt. Cocaine was never so vain as to offer a real answer to my problems. When I looked at her and she looked back at me, all she said was 'escape.' That's all I was looking for. I only bought Cocaine because I was uncomfortable with my numbness toward death. Death and I were well acquainted. I survived the un-survivable on more than one occasion. I was deeply bothered that Death would take so many of my people, and I was just wondering why he hadn't taken My Life. I figured I had a case of survivor's guilt, so I put my nose to my hand and inhaled hard. I knew I did it right when I felt that drip at the back of my throat.

I was awake in an instant, and all of a sudden it was like the world was listening to me. "Waymond's Song" came across the speakers as soon as I turned the truck back on. That's when I knew it was okay to drive home and get the party started. I shed no tears on the trip, but I was still Crying For Me on the inside. I wasn't sad that my friends were dead. I've always believed in death the same way Jim Morrison did: "People fear death more than pain. It's strange that they fear death. Life hurts a lot more than death. At the point of death, the pain is over." When we cry over death, those tears aren't shed for the dead. We cry for ourselves. We cry because we'll never see them again. The only ones that hear our tears are the living. Although I was okay with the idea of their death, I was hurt by the fact that I'd never tell sea stories with Jason again, that I'd never get the pleasant surprise of bumping into Jim at a bar when we were both drinking alone, and that never again would I be annoyed by the sound of Sandy's obnoxious laugh. They were dead, but they were better off than the rest of us. They were in the company of the greats, both famous and infamous. Those of us that were still alive had the most to worry about.

When I finally realized I wasn't driving anymore, I saw my coffee table and another carefully formed line in front of me, but it wasn't time yet. I had to do this right. I smoked a joint in silence in my bedroom with nothing but the bottle of bourbon to keep me company. I had to be high and drunk enough before I started. Once I was finished with the joint I went back into the living room. I pushed the coffee table away from the couch so I could sit on the floor between the two. That way I wouldn't have to lean all the way down from a seated position on the couch to do a line. When I took my seat, I made sure I had everything in their respective places, a loaded pipe on the right of the line and a filled shot glass on the left. When I was ready I hit the pipe and took the shot before I blew out the smoke. When I exhaled, the smoke hit the TV and billowed out into the room. When my lungs were empty I bent down and pressed a rolled twenty dollar bill to my nose. When I was sure the line was gone I tipped my head back and inhaled through my nose until the back of my throat tingled. The sensation hit me all at once. I had become Comfortably Numb.

I passed my night behind little white lines of escape. I sat in near darkness. I didn't need the overhead lights in the living room. The lights from outside were enough to see by, although they were dimmed by drawn blinds. I played music on my phone until the battery died – everything I could think of for any sad situation. The only other sounds in the room were snorts of cocaine, flicks of my lighter, and ignored vibrations of incoming text messages. I wanted to be sad and alone, but I couldn't push past pain to sadness. There was nothing in my mind that could make me shed a tear for my lost friends. I didn't understand why I'd simply let go of the loss so easily, especially when I had so much trouble moving past other losses. I guess it's easier losing someone to death than losing someone that's still alive.

I plugged my phone in to charge it when I saw the sun pushing through the blinds. I knew Portia was probably pissed. When the phone turned back on I had four unread messages from her. They read: "Hey, babe. What's going on." "Are you gonna be doing anything tonight, you should come over." "Is everything okay? I've been trying to get a hold of you but you're not responding." "I've tried calling. You're phone is on. What's going on? It's not like you to disappear like this."

I typed back, "I'm sorry I was out of touch last night. I had a really rough day yesterday. I've got to get ready for a funeral. Can I see you tonight? I'll explain everything then."

I did another line to wake up. I wasn't necessarily tired, but my mind knew that I needed some kind of sleep. It was more of a mental distress than any kind of fatigue. I had some cocaine left, but I saved it for another time. Showing up to a funeral with the cocaine sniffles was clearly a bad idea. I took a shower to sober up and I saw a missed call from Portia while I was drying off. I called her back as I got dressed.

"Are you okay?" she answered.

"I'm fine. I just got a lot of bad news yesterday. I needed to be alone."

"When's the funeral?"

"Eleven. It's at the church on Mass Ave. I'm leaving in a few minutes."

"I've got classes all morning, but I'll get someone to cover my night class. I should be home by two. Will I see you then?"

"As long as your eyes are open."

"Okay, baby. I love you."

I finished getting dressed when I got off the phone. If I took the time to look in a mirror, I probably would have been embarrassed about my appearance. I didn't work in a nice restaurant anymore, so my white button-ups and slacks weren't as well kept as they used to be. I threw them in the dryer for a few minutes, but that wasn't enough to completely knock out the wrinkles. They weren't really wrinkles anymore, they were more like the ghosts of wrinkles – variations in the texture and color of the fabric. Did it really matter? Would anyone say anything or even care at all? We weren't gathering to look good. We were gathering to say goodbye to a friend. I knew his parents and family wouldn't be at their best, and I figured I'd get all my points just for showing up. Although my shirt and slacks could have been better prepared, I made sure the tie looked good. That was one thing I still had control over.

It was a mile walk to the church, so I left the house at ten thirty. With mid-October came changing leaves, and the blend of autumn colors made living in the Maryland suburbs worthwhile. The sidewalk was a brown and orange mess of soggy leaves. The District of Columbia was constructed in reclaimed swamp land, and the early morning dew made the leaves sticky where they lay. When I came to the row of houses that lined the east side of Massachusetts Avenue, the layer of leaves was no longer consistent. Some home owners had already called their respective lawn services to come clean their yards, but no leaves were cleared across the property lines. The lines that separated the clean yards from the unclean yards were so straight it was almost like the lawn service had a surveyor come out and make sure they cleaned the entire yard without going an inch over the edge. Many home owners in the area had lawn services around the moment the leaves hit the ground.

People didn't appreciate the cycles of nature. People found the leaves of fall unsightly, but they failed to recognize their necessity. The trees rely on the death of fall to support the new life of spring.

When I got to the church, I saw my old work friends a few rows in. The service had just started so I took a seat in the back row to avoid interrupting anything. There wasn't a coffin. The family cremated the body and, after taking a look at the funeral program, I knew they were trying to get through everything as fast as possible. His parents each took a turn speaking. Some of his childhood friends had some time at the podium. His girlfriend, the person closest to him and the one that found him after he passed, was the last to go. She chuckled when she told us why there were two people standing behind her as she spoke – she was scared she'd pass out while she was speaking like she did when she found Jim dead in their apartment. I'd been in shoes similar to the ones she was wearing. Seeing a dead person really brings one's sense of mortality to the forefront. The thought of another's death reminds us of our own life and death. Life is finite, and, although it's nothing to dwell upon, it's still something to remember when you come face to face with a possible regret.

Her fear of fainting was unfounded. She did just fine. I wish I could tell you it was a beautiful service, but we all know that's just a lie we tell the family hoping it will ease their pain. Burying our dead is an ugly business, but we all have to do it. Birth and death are the only two things we all share – Christian, Jew, Muslim, Heathen, Gentile, and Infidel. No matter how hard we all try to fight it, one day we're all gonna get our turn. I'll admit, I've desired death on more than one occasion, but I know those that have never wanted to die never took the time to live in the first place.

The chapel emptied when Jim's girlfriend stepped down from the podium, and everyone went downstairs for a short wake. I gathered with my former work friends. Gerud shook my hand as I walked up and the girls took turns giving me a hug. Most of the people from the restaurant hadn't seen me since the afternoon I walked out in the middle of a shift. I felt bad for what happened, like I'd abandoned them, but no one held it against me that afternoon.

"It was so sudden," one girl said.

"I'm sorry you guys found out at work," I said.

"It was rough," another girl said. "A guy was so mean to me and I couldn't bring myself to tell him why I forgot to fill his water. The news about Jim spread when I went to grab the pitcher."

"You should have told me," Gerud said.

"I was still in shock."

"I think we're all in shock."

"Every life cut short is shocking," I said. The group went silent. Everyone but me looked at the ground. My gaze travelled from one pair of eyes to the next and the next and the next. Tears fell from men and women alike, but no one was free flowing. If someone cried, it was no more than a tear from each eye. They'd all gotten the heavy cries out of the way already.

After a moment of silence we shared a few stories. We tried to catch up on the six months that passed since I quit. Gerud and a couple others had seen me at the bar a few times, but most of them didn't even know where I was working. I enjoyed catching up on the restaurant gossip, who's sleeping with whom in the wine room and who can't seem to show up on what days. It was the same in every restaurant, but, no matter how many different places I worked, I couldn't get enough of it. I was never the subject of the gossip – I was smart enough to keep my personal life away from work – but I always made sure to keep up with the goings on. The restaurant world was reserved for those of us that could fit in anywhere but chose to fit in nowhere. It was the only real modern gypsy job outside the military, and there was no limit to the stupidity one could run into in even the nicest establishment. It was comforting to know the restaurant hadn't changed since I left.

The wake in the basement only lasted a few minutes before the group broke. A few of us gathered in the parking lot to smoke a cigarette before we went our separate ways. When I left the church, I didn't walk toward my apartment. I didn't want to lock myself up and spend the whole day on the floor in front of the couch like I had the night before. It was twelve o'clock and I was supposed to meet Portia in a couple hours. I needed to make sure that I didn't go crazy before then.

I wandered down some of the back streets, trying to stay away from Massachusettes Avenue. It made my walk to The University that much longer, but I didn't want to be in the public eye if I finally broke down like I wanted to.

Failing Aristotle

I didn't care about missing class, but I went to the library to email Dooshback and let her know why I skipped again. That wasn't the real reason I went to campus, but I figured it would be a good courtesy. When I was done in the library I walked outside and sat on a bench that faced the quad. The quadrangle was fifty yards wide and a couple hundred yards long. It was broken into parts by crossing sidewalks, but, other than that, it was a solid green patch. The north and south sides were lined with tall oak trees, but the leaves beneath them had already been cleaned up. I leaned forward with my elbows on my thighs and my tie hanging between my knees. That was when I realized that no one noticed the wrinkles in my shirt.

I looked out over the grass to watch the squirrels. I didn't know what it was about that particular rodent, but there's something about them that calmed me down. I've known since I was young that they were my spirit animal. I didn't need to go on the traditional spirit quest. They were an animal close to my own heart. Some people liked polar bears. Others liked pandas. I liked squirrels. It was more envy than anything else. I had to go through the day-to-day troubles of trying to survive while they spent their days solely in pursuit of getting a nut.

I don't know how long I sat at the bench watching the black squirrels chase the gray ones. Everywhere I lived before the District only had one kind of squirrel, so I never saw how aggressively racist squirrels were. A philosophy professor said to a class once that racism was an unnatural phenomenon, something uniquely human. I submitted the observation that squirrels tend to dislike one another based on the color of their fur. Although they don't see in true color, the difference in shades was still recognizable in grayscale. Black squirrels and gray squirrels hated each other. The gray ones were smaller and faster, so they stole food from the black squirrels. The black squirrels were bigger and stronger so they attacked the gray squirrels on sight. The University squirrels and their very human hatred for one another always lifted my spirit.

When I stood to leave, I paused before I walked anywhere. I saw Jessica across the quad. She was too far away to recognize me, but there was no mistaking her. I wanted someone to talk to, but I knew that talking to Jessica would only make things worse in the rest of my life. I wasn't even sure how to say 'hi' much less how to tell her about the events of the last twenty-four hours. I made it through an entire day alone, and I only had to survive the trip to Chinatown before I would see Portia again. Although I agreed to speak to Jessica if we saw one another, I made sure to stay out of her line of sight as I walked off campus.

When I finally got to Portia's apartment she was waiting for me by the door. "Are you okay?" she asked. "What happened?"

"The funeral today was for a friend I used to work with, but he wasn't the only person that died. I found out about three people yesterday."

"Oh no." She stepped in and pulled me back to her bedroom. Without saying a word she sat me down and got me ready for bed. She pulled the skinny end of the tie out of the knot and pulled it from around my neck. When the tie was neatly folded on the nightstand, she unbuttoned my shirt and pushed it down over my shoulders. The rolled sleeves fell right over my balled fists. Once I was topless, she pulled off my socks and shoes. Then she laid me down and pulled my slacks off. When she had me down to my underwear she righted me on the bed and lay down with me. She put my head on her shoulder and wrapped her arms around me, running her fingertips through the hair behind my ear.

"Who were they?"

"Friends and family."

"Tell me about them."

"The first person I heard about was Sandy, the closest thing I've had to a mom since my parents died. I've only seen her once in the better part of a decade. In one letter from home, I found out that she was diagnosed with lung cancer and that she died from the treatment. Some great family member I must be. Then there was an old co-worker named Jim. The last time I saw him I was doing cocaine off a toilet seat because he didn't want me to drive home drunk. He keeled over a couple days ago. We were the same age. We looked alike. We were almost the same person. That was the one that got to me most, but that wasn't the end to my bad news yesterday. Then I decided to look into a helicopter crash I heard about but never followed up on. That was when I found out about Jason. We went to boot camp and A-school together when we first joined the Navy. He died in Afghanistan last month. We lost touch when I left San Diego. I didn't even know he was married with a kid. Needless to say, it was a lot to get all at once and I didn't want to be alone tonight."

"You're Not Alone Tonight. I'm surprised you didn't call me last night. For a guy with 'No man is an island' tattooed on his arm, you're pretty closed off."

"After all the bullshit I went through growing up, it's a force of habit."

She rolled onto her side and her fingertips traced the three scars above my heart. "You told me."

"I kind of got used to death when I was watching the kids next to me drop like flies. At this point I just accept it. I know there's a part of me that just needs to let it all out. Last night, I scored some coke and a little weed and stayed up all night doing drugs trying to get emotional, but nothing ever came out. I must be some kind of cold-hearted the world has never seen."

"I don't think you're cold hearted. That's just the way you wanted to deal with it last night. But you're here now. I'm with you. I can see the pain hiding behind your eyes and I know you feel something. Through everything that happened to you as a kid you never took the time to learn the right way to feel, but that doesn't make you cold. It means you rationalize your way through pain."

"Is that healthy?"

"If it hasn't killed you yet, then it must be healthy for you."

"When I heard about my friend dying in Afghanistan, all I could think about was the fact that he wanted me to go to war with him. He wanted me right there beside him. I was glad I didn't say yes. I'm glad I wasn't on that helicopter with him."

"I'm glad, too, but you shouldn't think like that. That's not healthy."

"Sometimes I can't help what I think about. I really can't help but think that I'm never going to be anything more than a bartender."

"What do you want from life?"

"I just want an opportunity to live up to my potential."

"You can't expect the world to give you any opportunities. Sometimes you have to make your own luck."

"I'm working on that, but it always seems like the world doesn't want me to succeed. There's Gotta Be Something More."

"I spent a long time wanting something more than the life I was living, but then you came along. I love you, Michael, and I don't have to want any more than what I've got with you. You are so special to me and I don't have to try and be better than I am. You make me better. I don't find myself looking ten years down the road hoping I'm gonna find some great success. Most days it's nice to just be The Woman With You. I'm not saying you can't want something more, but you've got to learn to appreciate the things you have before you can pursue anything greater."

"I left home to conquer the world. I'm not exaggerating. I mean real life global conquest. But, since I left, I don't feel like I've accomplished anything real and I don't feel like I'm getting anything out of college."

"You're an amazing man. I hope you get to see that one day." She gripped my cheek and pulled me closer. That was when I noticed the water trapped between my cheekbone and her shoulder. I moved my head around beneath her hand in hopes she wouldn't notice the tear.

"Thanks for taking care of me tonight."

"That's what I'm here for, baby. I'll do anything for you."

"You promise?"

"Of course."

"Then hold me Like You'll Never See Me Again."

Chapter 7

"So what're you actually doing here?" Cait asked Holt from across the bar.

"Hopefully another Miller Lite and a shot of Jim Beam." Holt chuckled before he finished his beer, smiling wide as he set it on the bar mat in front of Cait.

Cait rolled her eyes as she stepped toward the beer cooler at the other end of the bar. She sat a fresh bottle and a shot glass in front of Holt. "You know what I mean. Why are you in New Jersey?"

"I told Mike – and I'm sure the two of you have talked about it since then – I came down here to trade signatures with Sera. She sent me divorce papers and I'm trying to close on selling the apartment. I can't do that without her signature because her name's on the title, too." Holt took the shot and slid the glass back across the bar toward Cait.

"Mike told me you showed up yesterday and started asking about Sera. But I was under the impression you two were supposed to sign the papers this morning."

"We thought it might be nice to talk a little before we rush through getting divorced. We haven't talked since she left. Are you trying to get rid of me?"

"No, I've missed you, if you can't tell. So has Mike. I haven't seen you in forever. But something isn't right. Sera has barely talked about you since she moved down here, and you show up out of nowhere. What's going on?"

"We're both seeing other people, and we're trying to be civil. Hell, maybe she and I will be friends when this is all over. I also thought it may be nice to see my two best friends in the whole wide world. Can't I just want to see you?"

Cait crossed her arms and cocked her head to the side. "Did you guys sign the papers today? Sera hasn't called me since she talked to you."

"Shouldn't you be paying attention to some of your other customers? If you spend all your time talking to me no one else is going to get any service."

"Stop dodging my question. I know how you work."

"No, we didn't."

"Thank God."

"Whoa…what's that all about?"

"Nothing." Cait picked up the shot glass and started walking toward the dishwasher at the far end of the bar.

"You can't yell at me for dodging questions and dodge one yourself."

"I've got customers to check on." Cait made her way down the bar. Holt turned in his stool to look for Mike. He was at the service station at the far end of the dining room floor. He was standing with one of the servers handling some issue or other. Holt worked in bars for years and he knew the types of mistakes that authoritative figures like Mike and Cait had to deal with on a nightly basis. It could have been server error – hitting the wrong button on the point of sale computer or forgetting that someone wanted a salad instead of French fries – or it could have been some asshole complaining about something stupid trying to get a free meal. Few people understood the level of accuracy to which those in the food service industry were held. If all industries were held to that same standard, a college student would get their entire education for free at the slightest dissatisfaction with their schooling or a president would be immediately fired if their approval rating fell below one hundred per cent. Holt was of the opinion that everyone should be required to work in restaurants because the job taught humility – and everyone needed to learn humility at some point.

As Mike walked away from the computer, he gave the young woman a pat on the shoulder. Mike was the type of guy that understood mistakes well because he was really good at making them. He believed that errors should be corrected rather than fingers pointed. In his industry there was no time to sit around and find someone to blame for every mistake. The key to being successful in restaurants was not avoiding mistakes; instead, it was the recognition of error and its correction before the snowball effect could take hold. The young lady Mike assisted was probably in the later stages of snowball growth because Mike walked toward a table only a few feet away to talk to the guests. His hands moved as he spoke and he looked from one guest to the next always maintaining eye contact. He was probably assuring them that everything was under control and offering to buy them another round of drinks while they waited for the server to right the error.

"Everything okay?" Holt asked when Mike walked back behind the bar. "You know I have no problem kickin' some ass up in this joint."

"You just stay right there in your seat, drink your beer, and let me deal with my guests."

"I thought I was a guest. You can't talk to me that way."

"You know where the door is…you need anything, brother?"

Holt looked through the darkened glass of his beer bottle. The beer was still just below the neck of the bottle. "I should be good for now."

Holt kept his gaze straight ahead as Mike moved away. There was a familiar face in the mirror behind the call liquors. Holt leaned forward, squinting to see the face a little clearer. He was unsure at whom was he was looking, so he turned to get a better picture. It looked like-

"That cunty bitch."

Sera walked through the front door with some guy Holt did not recognize. He was almost as tall as Holt, but he was a lot skinnier. The look on his face was one of boredom, and the guy's stature screamed uninteresting. "How dare she."

Holt righted himself in the seat. He looked toward the far end of the bar where Mike and Cait were standing together. Cait's eyes were wide and her gaze darted back and forth between Holt and Sera as she whispered something in Mike's ear. Mike looked over his shoulder and Holt could read clearly the "Oh Fuck" on his lips when he saw Holt, Sera, and Sera's new boyfriend in the same room. Mike walked back toward Holt, taking his time and smiling from ear to ear. The only problem was that Mike never smiled. "Hey, buddy, how ya doin'?"

"Shot…Double…Please," Holt mumbled through grinding teeth. Mike turned to pour Holt a glass of whiskey and Cait darted around the bar toward Sera.

"Holt, you better play nice. The two of you are getting divorced and she comes in here all the time with Matt."

"Fuck that. This was my bar long before it was hers."

"This is my bar – not yours. You haven't been in here in a while. She's in here a couple times a week. She's more than welcome here."

"I'm not pissed that she's here. I'm pissed that she came here with him." Holt downed the rocks glass full of whiskey in one gulp and slid

the glass back across the bar as he'd done with the shot glass a few minutes before. This time, however, he had to take a long pull on his beer to chase the triple shot of bourbon. "Hell, just a minute ago your wife thanked God we hadn't signed our divorce papers. What the hell was that all about?"

"Couldn't tell you."

"Bullshit." Holt leaned in closer to Mike and tried to keep his voice low. "She can't come in here with her new boyfriend when she knows I'm gonna be in here. That's so fucking mean."

"I don't think she's doing this with any kind of malice," Mike responded.

"It doesn't change the fact that it hurts. What a bitch." Holt pursed his lips, looking up and left toward nothing. His wheels turned for a couple seconds before he continued, "I'm gonna fuck someone – someone hotter than Sera. That'll make me feel better. Maybe then she'll know how I feel."

"Holt, please trust me when I say that fucking someone else tonight will not do any good for your situation. Why don't you and I get out of here and smoke a joint. Cait's got this for the night."

"I'll leave when I've got someone on my arm." Holt finished his beer and pushed his stool away from the bar. "I'm gonna step outside and cool off."

Mike set a coaster on top of the empty bottle. "I'm gonna do a lap and I'll meet you out there."

Holt mean-mugged Sera as he stood, but he kept his gaze elsewhere as he walked toward the door. He fished for his phone in his pocket to try and call Alex. She would know what to say to calm him down by the time Mike made it outside. He found her name in the contact list. He looked toward the door as the phone started ringing, but a sexy red dress stole his attention from the phone call.

The red dress was wrapped around an angel of a higher order, an angel whose light outshone any in the room. He glanced at her as he walked, but he was careful to ignore her as they passed each other. The snapshot in his head was more than enough. She was tall, sandy blond, and she looked like she could have been a centerfold. Her dress started in narrow straps over firm, tanned, chewable shoulders. Although the dress was skin tight, the straps pulled away from her body just below

51

her shoulders but contact with her skin resumed as the straps widened over her bust. Finally the straps came together in a low-cut v leaving little to imagine about her chest. The skirt narrowed around her waist – the contours of her stomach visible through the fabric. The difference between her waist and her hips must have been at least fourteen inches. The dress ended no less than two inches below her crotch, but her muscular thighs continued none the less. She wasn't a body builder by any means, but her thighs flexed as she walked. Her calves looked just soft enough to sit on either side of Holt's head while she was on her back, but her spiked heels made them look strong enough to break his neck. A woman only dressed like that when she wanted to get noticed.

Not many women in the world could distract a man enough he forgot he was calling a fuck buddy – especially one as hot as Alex. Holt finally remembered he was on the phone when Alex's voicemail answered the call. After the beep he said, "I'm out at my friends' bar and I saw Sera with her new boyfriend. I was just hoping you could calm me down, but you're probably busy. Talk to you soon."

"Who you calling?" Mike asked as he walked outside and lit up.

"Doesn't matter." Holt ended the call and stuffed his phone back in his pocket. His eyes went wide and he smiled as he looked back at Mike. "Did you see the girl in the red dress?"

"Everyone saw the girl in the red dress."

"I think I'm in love," he said as he unbuttoned one of his sleeves and folded it up his forearm.

"I don't think you should waste your time on that one. She's way out of your league."

"I think that makes her exactly my type," Holt responded as he finished rolling up his sleeves. "I see my wife with her new boyfriend and the hottest girl in the world walks into the bar. Why would I waste an opportunity like that?" Holt looked past Mike toward the bar. "She's sitting down next to me. It must be fate."

"Fate won't get her attention and you aren't that pretty. How the hell are you gonna land a girl like that?"

Holt looked down at his recently exposed tattoos before pushing past Mike and walking inside. "I've already done all I have to do, sir."

When Holt sat back down at the bar, he kept his eyes straight forward. His strategy was simple, he ignored her. It was obvious that she wanted to be noticed, and every eye in the bar was pointed straight at her. Not staring would make him stand out against the crowd.

"What'll it be?" Mike asked as he walked up to the woman in the red dress.

"I'll have a vodka martini, straight up."

"With olives or a twist?" Mike asked as he pulled a Martini glass off the shelf. He filled it with ice and soda water to chill it before making her drink.

"Olives…and can you make it dirty?" She turned her head as she spoke. Holt was running his hand through his hair, and the tattoo on his right forearm caught her attention. Old tactics were always the best ones. Holt smiled at Mike as Mike emptied the ice and club soda out of the martini glass to make room for the drink he prepared.

"Would you like to see a menu?" Mike asked as he strained the martini into the glass.

"Just drinking tonight."

"It'll be five."

"Dollars?" She handed Mike her credit card. "That's amazing."

"It's always happy hour here at Happy Hour and everything's on special. You wanna close it out or leave it open?"

"Open." Holt thanked God inside his head as she said the magical I'm-not-going-anywhere-for-a-while word.

"I'll give this right back to you." Mike stepped away to open her tab and she looked at Holt's tattoo again as he took a drink.

"What does that mean?" she asked.

Holt turned to look at her as her green eyes scanned up and down the tattoo on his forearm. "What?" he pretended not to know what she was asking about.

She ran her finger across his tattoo. "I think it's Latin. 'Est' is 'is' but I don't know the rest."

"Ah." Holt slid his half rolled sleeve the rest of the way up his forearm to expose the rest of the tattoo. He held his arm up so she could read the whole tattoo and said, "The die is cast."

"The die is cast," she echoed. "Like dice?"

"Yeah. The story is that Julius Caesar spoke those words as he crossed the Rubicon River which separated his consulship from Pompeii's. Under Roman law, the crossing was a declaration of war on

53

the Senate and Pompeii. He became an outlaw and he had to follow through to the finish – whether it meant victory or death. Just like you can't know what the result is going to be until the dice have finished rolling."

"And what's that one?" she asked, pointing to his left arm.

"This one's in English." He turned in his stool and moved a little closer to her.

She took his forearm in her hand and read, "It was the best of times, it was the worst of times…" She pulled him out of his seat. "…it was the age of wisdom, it was the age of foolishness…" She twisted his arm as she read the long line of prose coiled around his arm. "…it was the epoch of belief, it was the epoch of incredulity…" Holt had to turn his body as she read. "…it was the season of Light, it was the season of Darkness…" As she read Holt looked in the mirror behind the bar again and again. "…it was the spring of hope, it was the winter of despair…" He was standing now, and he could see the reflection of the bar behind him much better than earlier. "…we had everything before us, we had nothing before us…" Sera was looking straight at him. "…we were all going direct to heaven, we were all going direct the other way…" Holt and Sera stared one another down through the mirror. "…in short, the period was so far like the present period…" Neither looked away as the woman in the red dress manipulated Holt's arm to read. "…that some of its noisiest authorities insisted on its being received…" Matt had no idea as he tried to get Sera's attention. "…for good or for evil, in the superlative degree of comparison only."

When the woman in red finished reading she asked, "Isn't that Charles Dickens?"

"It's the first sentence in <u>A Tale of Two Cities</u>. It's the longest sentence I know of. I've never made it through the entire novel but I've always loved this sentence."

"Why get the tattoo if you've never read the whole book?"

"Because it's so perfectly timeless." He pointed to the phrase near the end of the sentence. "Right here when he writes 'the period was so far like the present.' It connects the modern days to the Victorian era the same way it connected the Victorian era to the time of the French Revolution."

"For someone who hasn't read the book you seem to know a lot about it."

"It's my job to know."

"And what is it you do?"

"I'm a writer. But I also work as an agent in my spare time."

"Any other tattoos?"

"I've got another one in Latin on my right arm." Holt turned his arm over so she could see. "It means 'Fortune favors the bold.' That's all I can show you here. I have to take some clothes off if you want to see the rest of them." Holt was careful to maintain eye contact while he spoke to her. The easiest way to alienate a woman of her caliber was to get caught staring at her tits. Although he kept his eyes on hers, he still did everything he could to study the perfection that lay beneath that skin-tight, red dress. After taking in the sight for a quiet moment, he held out a hand to introduce himself. "I'm Holt."

"Catherine. But my friends call me Cat."

"You have any tattoos?"

She turned in her stool and put her back to Holt. On the back of her shoulder there was an image of a man holding a jar, and the jar was tipped so its contents poured out. Even though it only took a second to examine the small tattoo, he took a little extra time to examine the shoulder as a whole. She was thin, but not bony. She was muscular enough he could see the contours of her deltoids but only when the muscles contracted. Although the tattoo fit the shoulder well, it was still like putting a bumper sticker on a Maserati. "What is it?" Holt asked.

"It's my birth sign. I'm an Aquarius."

"This guy bothering you?" Mike asked, standing with his arms crossed and his chest out. He spoke from the diaphragm to sound harder than he really was. Catherine's drink was already getting low. "I'll kick him out. All you have to do is say the word."

"I can handle myself."

"Would you like another martini?"

"Yes, please."

"Throw that one on my tab, sir," Holt interrupted.

"You don't have to do that," she cut in.

"I insist. As a rule I usually don't buy girls drinks at bars, but I think I can make an exception tonight." Mike rolled his eyes as he walked away to make her drink.

"A man with a code," she said as she finished her first drink. "Why break the rules tonight?"

"Because any man that wouldn't buy a girl like you a drink is either gay or retarded."

Catherine laughed and smiled and looked at the floor and back at Holt. Flattery usually sat outside Holt's repertoire, but he broke it out on rare occasions. "What do you write?"

"I'll admit that I'm more of an agent than a writer these days. I've written one novel, but it's never been published."

"What's it about?"

"The same thing as every shitty, first novel: men and women, everything and nothing."

"Your girlfriend must be quite the lady to inspire a whole novel."

"I'm actually getting divorced. I'm in New Jersey signing the papers. But that was quite the good job of fishing for my relationship status. Your boyfriend must be terrified of your interrogation skills."

She bit her upper lip and popped her eyebrows. "I, too, am recently single – not divorced though. I'd been dating a guy for a couple years and, like most cliché endings, he turned out to be a cheating piece of shit. I thought he was the one, but it's time I accept the fact that I deserve better."

"Moving on is the hardest part."

"Moving on was easy," she turned on her stool so her legs mixed with Holt's, "but getting ready to move wasn't. For a long time I thought it was impossible."

"You know I'm totally stealing that from you."

"I give you permission." She leaned closer.

"Let's find a brighter subject." He smiled a half smile.

"Like your book. Can I read it?"

"I don't have it with me. My copy is back at my hotel."

"I'd love to read it sometime, but I guess I'll just have to wait for you to publish it."

"We'll have to see, won't we?" Holt finished another beer and set it on the bar mats. Cait saw the empty and brought Holt a fresh one.

"Are you talking about <u>Failing Aristotle</u>?" she asked as she set the beer down. "I didn't know you still had a copy."

"I rewrote it a while back to give it to Sera – that's my ex," he said aside to Catherine before turning back to Cait, "but I never got the chance before it all ended."

"What about the rest of it?" Cait asked.

"There's more?" Catherine interrupted.

"I didn't know that part well enough to rewrite it."

"Oh," Cait's voice fell as she turned to walk to Mike.

"Enough about the book I'll probably never publish. What do you do for a living?"

Catherine was already leaning back. She rimmed the top of her martini with her index finger. Her other arm was extended with her hand resting on the back of Holt's bar stool. "I'm a physical therapist. I specialize in personal training and sports rehabilitation."

"You must give one hell of a backrub."

"Oh, I do." She looked from Holt to the almost empty martini and back at Holt.

"I haven't had a good massage in a long time."

"I'll give you a back rub if you let me read your book. Does that sound fair?"

"If I let you read the whole book I'll never get my backrub."

"I'll give you a backrub if you let me read a chapter."

"Deal. I can run back and grab the book."

"I'll just go with you if that's okay."

"I'm not opposed."

She slid off the stool and smoothed her dress after she was standing. "I'm gonna use the little girls' room before we go."

"I'll settle us up. If I'm not here when you get back, meet me outside." Holt made the universal check mark in the air when Mike looked over.

"You rewrote your book?" Mike asked as he set down Holt's check.

"Just my half."

"You think that rewriting it would get your wife back? It wasn't even about her."

"I rewrote it before she left. We were on the rocks and it was the only way I could think to deal with it. It was the reason she fell in love

57

with me, and I thought seeing it again might help us work things out. She left before I had the chance to give it to her." Holt signed his check and stood to leave. "You ever think about writing again?"

"Published or no I consider what I wrote a success. I got my wife out of it."

"I never doubted the two of you would wind up together. You two have always been a beautiful mess – perfectly imperfect for one another."

"Have a good night, brother." Mike shook Holt's hand across the bar.

Holt only made it one step before he stopped and turned back to Mike. "Before I go, Sera and Phil are having a bar-be-que tomorrow. Will you be my date? I've got a plus one I can't fill."

"You're not gonna take the porn star?"

"She's a physical therapist, but, don't worry, you're the only woman for me."

"Get the fuck outta here. I'll call you in the morning."

Holt walked toward the door and took a long look at Sera as he passed. Her half of the table had twice as many empty beer bottles as her date's half.

After Catherine met Holt outside, they turned to walk toward his hotel. Cat crossed her arms right after they started moving. The breeze off the water was strong enough it whistled in Holt's seaward ear. Halfway to the hotel Cat said, "I'm cold." He took the hint to put his arm around her bare shoulders. He warmed her for the rest of the short walk, but he had to step away to open the front door of the hotel. They finished the walk through the lobby and up the wide stairwell side by side. When they got to the room, he pulled his book out of the backpack.

"I guess I'll give you two some privacy," Holt said as he handed her the book and started toward the balcony.

"I'll come get you when I'm finished," she said as he walked outside.

He lit a cigarette and watched the empty beach. He could hear the roar of the waves from what must have been more than a hundred yards away, the sound of the rising tide carried by the wind. He tried to keep his mind on the waves, but his thoughts kept running back to the woman in his room. Looking inside would just make her feel awkward while she read, so he kept his back to the sliding door. She was probably on the couch or sitting in the chair with the book open in front of her. Her body would be leaning forward and her cleavage would look even better than it did when they were sitting together at the bar. If Holt was in the room with her he would have tried to catch a peak up her dress as she adjusted her crossed legs. Sure, he would probably see anything he wanted to see soon, but patience was a difficult concept to wrap his head around when his next mate would make Aphrodite self conscious.

"I love your writing." Cat's voice drowned out the sound of the sliding glass door and the words pulled Holt toward her. He turned without hesitation or response. Instead, he walked with fast, heavy feet toward her as she pulled the door shut. "I love the title to the first chapter. What does it mean: 'Soundtrack 2 my Life'?"

He stopped when he realized she asked a question, pausing and shaking off his desire to tackle her through the balcony door. "All the chapter titles are song titles," he responded. "I thought that one was the best title to start with. You know, hinting that it's a soundtrack."

"Clever." She leaned back against the glass door and bit her lip. "How 'bout that backrub?"

"What about it?"

"I thought that was the deal," She slid the door open and stepped back through, "one chapter for one backrub."

"That was the idea," Holt responded as he followed her inside.

"Take off your shirt," she said as she walked into the bathroom. He was hanging his shirt on the back of the desk chair when she came back out. She had a small bottle of lotion in her hand.

He walked to the foot of the bed and stood facing her. When she was a few feet away from him, she squinted a little and leaned forward and walked closer. Something on Holt's shirtless chest caught her eye. She stopped just in front of him, leaning in to read the small tattoo. She ran her fingers across the ink as she read. "'True to thyself.' I really like the script."

"It's the only freehand tattoo I've got. I got it right after my parents and my brother died – I'm sorry if that's an over share."

"Don't be sorry. I'm sorry you lost your parents."

"It was fifteen years ago, so I'm pretty used to the whole orphan thing. Anyway, the real quote comes from Hamlet, and it's 'To thine own self be true,' but I made this one mine when I set out to conquer the world at eighteen."

"How's that going for you?"

"It was going great until I messed everything up."

"I'm sure you'll get everything figured out." She patted his chest with an open palm. "Get on the bed."

"Yes, ma'am."

She stepped out of her heels as Holt lay down. He rolled onto his stomach and she straddled him, taking a seat on his butt. She started rubbing lotion all around his back and her hand lingered when she started rubbing his right shoulder blade.

"Why do you have a cross tattooed on your back?"

"We all have our crosses to bear. Mine's just heavier than most and I need a reminder every once in a while."

"And what is this cross you bear?"

"I already told you…I'm supposed to conquer the world."

"Why are you supposed to conquer the world?"

"Because I can. Because it needs to be conquered."

"That's a lot of pressure to put on yourself."

"You have no idea. That's why my back is so messed up."

"You have a lot of knots." When she found a knot she pressed down so hard she lifted off him. "You're back is like one big knot. How long has it been since someone worked on your back?"

"Since before my wife and I split up. Probably a year."

"You carry a lot of tension along your spine."

"Working at a desk will do that to you."

"I don't think I can work all of these knots out in one session."

"I wouldn't expect you to. You really don't have to rub my back if you don't want to."

"Maybe I was trying to undress you so I could see the rest of your tattoos. Besides, I once heard that two-thirds of all massages end in sex."

"I'm not going to do something just because everyone else is doing it. I don't like living inside statistics."

"That's a shame." She leaned down, whispering so close to his ear that he could feel her lips moving against it. "I thought this was a sure-fire way to seduce you."

"You've already said the magic words. I woulda jumped your bones on the balcony, but you really wanted to give me a massage."

"What were the magic words?"

"I'm not gonna just tell you." Holt turned over so he was supine. He smiled up at her with narrowed eyes. "Then this wouldn't be any fun for me."

She raised her head, twisting it and looking into the corner of the room as she thought. Holt's hands were on her thighs and he could feel her heating up. They were so close. If pre-foreplay was this hot, what would the moment of climax be like? Not only was this woman hot as hell, she actually had a decent personality – a rarity among the hot ones. Sure, they went home together on the first night, but only a fool would pass up on an opportunity with her. She was rebounding and Holt needed someone with whom to sleep. Seeing his wife with another guy made him sore, and the best medication for his pain was thinking on the other side of the red dress.

About the time Holt thought he was gonna lose it early, she bit her lower lip and looked down at him. "I know what it is."

"I don't think you do."

"Oh...I do." She looked down and ran her fingers across the tattoo on his chest. "You really are a writer at heart."

"What makes you say that?"

"I love your writing."

Colder Weather

She'd trade Colorado if I took her with me, but she closed the door on us before the winter of our despair let the cold in. Once upon a time, she wondered if her love was strong enough to make me stay. She was answered by my taillights shining through her window pane. Although Jess and I were in no danger of getting back into a relationship in the immediate future, the idea of saying goodbye was out of the question. Neither of us wanted to lose the other, but I didn't think I could survive her friendship much longer. I definitely had a couple bruised ribs, but none were broken. My face was pretty busted up. My shirt was torn half way down the front. It was a hell of a fight I'd gone through for her, but you should've seen the other guy – actually, guys if I remembered right. The pounding on the right side of my forehead was getting in the way of my memory, and it felt an awful lot like a footprint. I needed a drink.

As I walked along Western Avenue toward Friendship Heights, I tried to rub all the spots that hurt. Only problem was that I didn't have enough hands to rub everything at once. There was a bar ten minutes up the street, but I was walking at the speed of fucked up. That added ten extra minutes. I wasn't heading toward the bar at which I'd started the night, but a bar was a bar by that point. My phone rang, but my head hurt too much to focus on the phone and walking simultaneously. I had to stop to answer.

"Where are you?" It was Jessica.

"I'm walking down Western. I'm trying to get to Chadwick's before last call."

"I can't believe you stayed behind to fight them."

"It wasn't much of a fight. I kicked the shit out of them and they landed a few when they got an opportunity."

"There were five of them. What were you thinking?"

"They didn't look that big. Only one had any real size. He went down pretty fast though. Then I only had four to deal with."

"Are you crazy?"

"That's obvious. Just come and get me." I ended the call and took a seat on the curb to wait. I checked the street to make sure I wouldn't get hit, but there was no one on the road. Washington had a tendency of shutting down after midnight – even on the weekends. I lit a cigarette and watched both ends of the street as I waited for Jessica to show up with my truck. There was blood stained on the butt as I held it between my fingers. It tasted sweet as I licked the stain from my lips and stubble.

Jessica's eyes went wide when she saw me. When I opened the door my head was low and my eyes were fixed on the Angel Without Wings in the driver's seat.

"Thank you," she said as I got in.

"For what, letting you drive my truck?"

"For coming through. My boyfriend wasn't there and you were when you didn't have to be. I can't thank you enough."

"Yeah, you can. Dump his ass so we can get back together."

"I'm not going to hurt him like that. Besides, I thought you were still dating that girl."

"Portia? I wouldn't really call it dating. We haven't seen each other before ten o'clock at night."

"Gee, thanks for the visual."

"I'm only sleeping with her because I finally got tired of waiting for you. You have no one to blame but yourself."

We finished the drive back to her house in silence. I laid the seat back and tried to breathe as little as possible – the only thing worse than a bruised ribcage was a broken one. The bruises made everything hurt because everything involved breathing. I couldn't talk without a pain following the sound up my throat and out my mouth. I couldn't walk because it felt like Wild Horses trampling me from my nipples to my knees. I jerked my eyes open before I fell asleep. I looked at Jessica. She was focused on driving and wasn't paying attention to the fact that I probably had a concussion.

Jessica parked around the back side of her apartment. She got out of the truck and raced around to help me out. I was half out the door by the time she got to me, and she worked her shoulder under my arm as I closed the door. I tried not to put my weight on her, but the bruises up and down my left flank made it hard for me to support my own weight. It must have been the rest in the truck that made it worse. Everything had a chance to get stiff.

She helped me up the stairs toward the back entrance. "The right side of your head is one big bruise. Is that a footprint?" she asked as she held the door open for me.

"I think so."

Jessica had both her hands on me for support, and I used my right arm to support myself on her shoulders. I had to press the up-button with my broken left hand.

"I thought you said you won that fight," she said as she helped me onto the elevator.

"No one wins a fight, but I lost less than they did." I propped myself up on the railing inside the elevator. She didn't have to support my weight, so she took the time to rub some sore muscles with her free finger tips. She knew better than most how much I liked to have my back scratched. Instead of telling her where to move her scratching hand, I pressed my head into the wall and moved my back around under her nails.

"You're like a cat," she said with a smile.

"Don't scratch so hard." She found another bruise concealed beneath my ripped shirt.

"Wow. I think that's the first time you've ever told me to scratch softer."

"Hopefully it'll be the only time, too."

"C'mon. It's not far to my apartment." She pulled me off the elevator wall and pushed me through the opening door. "We can put you on the couch and ice some of those bruises when we get there. I think I still have one of your shirts, too. That way we can get rid of the one you're wearing."

"What shirt do you have?"

"That one I stole from you when we met."

"You know, I've only worn that shirt twice. You've worn it more than I have. You used to sleep in it all the time."

"I still do every now and then. You were wearing it the night we met. It means a lot to me."

"Is that why you stole it?"

"It's one of the reasons."

"What are the other reasons?"

"That's not important."

"Humor me, please. I'm in pain."

She looked at the floor before she answered. "I like how it smells, a little whiskey mixed with sweat and cigarette smoke – like you."

"What does your boyfriend think about you keeping my shirt?"

"It's really easy to hide things in a long distance relationship. He has no idea."

"That doesn't strike you as a bad sign on your part."

"I'm not having this conversation again. Can we focus on the fact that you can't stand instead of the fact that I'm in a relationship with someone else."

I lifted myself off her shoulder when we got to her door. I walked to the far side and made sure I stood under my own weight. The pain was excruciating, but I managed to hide my hurt behind a flat expression. "Although it feels good to be taken care of, don't think I need you to nurse me back to health right now. I can manage if I have to."

"I didn't mean it like that. I just meant that I don't want to talk about our lack of relationship right now. It gets kind of old after a while."

"Being friends with the former love of my life got old a long time ago." She held the door open and I walked past. "But I've been doing it for almost a year now, even if I haven't done the best job of it." By the time I finished speaking I was half-way across the living room, looking back at Jess over my shoulder. Out of the corner of my eye I could see she wasn't moving. She was still holding the door open as I turned to face her. "Fine, I'll drop it."

"Thank you." She let the door go as she walked toward the kitchen. "Take your shirt off. I'll be right back."

I tried to lift the shirt over my head but I couldn't lift my hands above my shoulders. The muscles along my ribs couldn't stretch far enough. I heard Jess cracking ice trays in the kitchen as I debated how to get my shirt off without help. She was on a high and mighty trip because she found a way she could help me for once – that always made her feel special because I was very self-sufficient. I wasn't giving her the satisfaction of helping me out with my shirt. I surveyed the tear. The nylon collar was already ripped and that was the hardest part to get through. When Jessica came out of the kitchen, I was wincing in pain as I finished the rip down the front, pulling the shirt down my arms.

"I could've helped you with that."

"Ah…shit." My chest was in no shape to stretch as I worked the sleeves over my wrists. "See? I got it."

"Lie down." She rolled her eyes as she pushed me toward the couch. Before I could turn around and lie down she stopped me. She stepped in close. My chin and her forehead were at the same height, so she only had to hunch a little to put her eyes even with my chest. "What's that?"

"What are you talking about?"

"I've never seen this tattoo. When did you get it?"

"I got it when I went to Kansas over Spring Break. You were in Florida and I knew exactly what was going on. I fell apart when I realized I'd pushed you into a relationship with someone else. That was when I realized I needed to start getting my life back together. I guess it's been a while since you've seen me with my shirt off."

"It has." She glanced toward my eyes and back to my chest, tracing her finger across the tattoo as she did every time she saw fresh ink on my skin. I looked over my shoulders to make sure we were alone. Her roommate was passed out from the roofie, but, still, I checked to make sure the bedroom door was shut. There was a neurosis that came with our intimacy. God forbid anyone find out we were still so close. Moreover, I had to make sure no one saw how much I still loved the way her hands felt against my skin. "'True to thyself.' I approve. I love the way the capital T curls around the scar. Like the word 'True' is holding the scar there."

"I didn't even notice when I first got the tattoo. The scars on my shoulder, my knee, and my forehead are so visible, but the three on my chest are tough to notice. I forget they're there sometimes. Low and behold, I was moisturizing the tattoo a couple days after I got it and I saw how well the tattoo fit together with the scars. It's almost poetic."

"Of all the ink and scars you have, those are the three marks that most define you."

"I'm just glad those scars never faded – some of my lesser scars have. If I ever lost those there'd be no proof that I'm a good person."

"You've always been a good person. You're the only person who has trouble believing that."

"I'm workin' on it."

"All you have to do is remember that you gave your wish away. I don't know anyone else that's ever done anything so selfless." She put both her hands flat on my chest, rubbing the scars one last time. "Get on the couch. Let me take care of you."

"Wrap this around the ice bag so I don't get frostbite." I handed her what was left of my shirt before I lowered myself face down on the couch.

"I think you should go to the hospital. You look like you were on the losing end of a bad Chuck Norris joke."

I tried to laugh, but I had to pull one of my hands out from under my head to hold my ribs. "I'd karate chop Chuck Norris right in his beard. Besides, I've had enough trouble with hospitals. I can't afford to go."

"What am I gonna do with you?" she asked as she took a seat.

"Nurse me back to health so I can go back to work in a couple days."

"At least you have a couple days off to heal. Hopefully the bruises on your face go away."

"The bruises on my face will make for a great story behind the bar. I'm more worried about my ribcage. How am I supposed to lift a keg if I have to change one?"

"You'll just have to pray they don't kick."

"Speaking of kicks, how long were you thinking up that Chuck Norris thing?"

"What are you talking about? You're not the only witty person in the room."

"But that's not really your style. C'mon, tell me."

"I started working on it about the time I carried you up the stairs out back. I had to wait for the right opportunity."

"I knew it...I haven't been in this bad've shape since before the Navy. I was helping my brother break a mean little filly and I got bucked off. I picked myself up and we chased her out into the field. When we got close she saw me comin' and kicked the shit out of me. I must've flown twenty feet before I hit the ground. You think the shoe print on my face is bad. You could see the nails in the horseshoe imprinted on my chest after that one."

"You still haven't told me what it was like seeing him after eight years."

"He's still a little upset that I left the way I did after mom and dad died and I –"

"– left the way you did."

"In a nutshell." I pulled my hands out from under my head, resting my cheek on the couch cushion. "You're the only thing I've never left behind. That's why I went home after being gone so long. I can drop anything and move on, but I can't let you go like that."

"I don't want you to let go."

"You let go."

"What makes you think that?"

"The fact that you've been in a relationship with someone else for five months. The emotional ambiguity in every statement you make. The fact that you still don't know what you want. The ambivalence in your eyes right now."

"You're not looking at my eyes."

"I don't have to. If you haven't let go there's only two possibilities: either you're telling him you love him because you're hiding from the true love you feel for me, or you're making me hold on to keep your options open. Who showed up tonight? Who fought to defend your roommate's honor? It's been a fight to stay in your life, but I don't have any fight left. I didn't stay to fight those guys for honor. I stayed to feel something. And I stayed to burn off some of the anger that I've bottled up over this stupid situation we're in. And it is stupid…if you really haven't moved on."

"Maybe we should take some time apart so we can both see."

"See what?"

"If we've moved on."

"Are you serious?"

"Isn't that what you want?"

"What I want has never mattered. We can take time apart, but it's gonna be because you want it."

She didn't make a sound as I force my way around her and sat up. All of a sudden the pain in my chest and head didn't seem so painful. It was all superseded by a pain growing inside my heart.

"I guess that is what I want" she said as she broke the long silence. "I'd like to see what it's like without you around every day. You know, see if I really am happy with the new life I've chosen. But this isn't over between us."

"It's not?"

She said, "I want to see you again. But I'm stuck in…"

"You want to take time apart, but this isn't over. What is it you really want from all this?"

"I don't know what I want. That's the problem. All I know is that I don't want this to be goodbye. Let's set a date to talk. Let's get together on 11-11-11 just to make sure we don't lose touch."

"So we're taking time apart just to see one another again. That doesn't really sound like an attempt at moving on."

"It's not moving on. It's just seeing what moving on is going to feel like."

"What do you think it's going to feel like?"

"I don't know, but I want to know whether or not I'm actually going to like it. I like having you around. I like all our crazy conversations – all your stories. You're a brilliant person and you can talk about anything at any time. I don't want to lose that with you, but you don't sound like you're happy anymore."

"I haven't been happy since we broke up. I've been talking about taking time apart since then and you've been guilting me into staying friends with you. I think it's quite the coincidence that I start seeing someone else and you decide that you want to take time apart. I've had to sit by while you've been dating someone else but you can't handle it when I start to." I stood up and walked toward the door. She chased after me holding the shirt she stole.

"You should take this," she said as she offered the shirt to me. For two people that broke up almost a year and a half earlier, this was starting to sound an awful lot like a break up.

"I don't want it anymore," I said, stopping short of the door. "It'll just make me think of you. You can throw it away if you don't want it."

"I never throw away the Memories Of Us." That all changed on her birthday.

"I guess I'll see you in a couple months." I didn't even turn to look at her as I spoke.

She stopped me as I opened the door to leave. "Don't I at least get a hug before you go?"

"No." I cupped my hand on the side of her face to comfort the denial. "You'll be fine."

When I walked out of the door and down the hall, I didn't look back. It was the first time I walked away from her not caring if I'd ever see her again. For once in my life I felt like I was moving on without running away. This was a new beginning like none other. With every step away from her door her gravity faded and I got A Little Bit Stronger. By the time I got to my truck, I didn't even hurt anymore.

I started the truck and called Portia before I pulled out of the parking spot. "You down for that rain check?" I asked when she answered.

"I'm about to head back to my place. Come. But I gotta warn you, I've had a bit to drink."

"I'm a little messed up myself."

It was a long, downhill trip along Massachusetts Avenue toward Chinatown. Massachusetts was nothing but apartment buildings and parks until I crossed Wisconsin Avenue, the main artery from the suburbs into Georgetown. Then I passed the National Cathedral on my left and I followed the curve of the road around the Naval Observatory on my right. I checked the time as I past the Navy Master Clock display at the Observatory entrance. It was officially one in the morning. Just past the observatory I passed the British embassy. It was one of the largest foreign compounds in the city. Right after I passed the statue of Winston Churchill at the far end of the embassy, I crossed the bridge over Rock Creek Parkway and entered Embassy Row. These embassies were smaller. These were the Isles of Man, Peru, Chile, and Spain. If it wasn't for all the foreign flags lining both sides of the street, I would have thought Embassy Row was a bunch of row houses.

During rush hour, Massachusetts was bumper to bumper, but when there was no traffic on the road, I could drive from outer Bethesda to RFK Stadium in half an hour. It was a great drive when no one else was on the road, and all I had to do was let gravity do all the work. Other than the occasional red light, I only had to slow down for one part of the drive. Dupont Circle was the center of a large bar district and most of the village idiots thought it was a good idea to cross against the light in the middle of blinding, late-night traffic.

Once I got to Chinatown I had to drive around to find parking. My truck wasn't designed to be driven in a metropolitan area, so I had to find enough room to park one and a half cars. When I finally found parking, I was five blocks from Portia's place. I sent her a text when I got out of my truck, but I paused to finish the cigarette I smoked on the walk before I buzzed her apartment. I couldn't wait to see her reaction, but I had to prepare myself before I walked up the stairs. We weren't really dating at that point, but we spent a lot of time together. We were both off on Tuesday and Thursday nights, so those days were religiously blocked off. If any other night freed up we were always the first on each other's call lists. Sometimes, I'd even roll by on the weekends when I got off work at two or three in the morning. She always said our schedules were quite fortunate for our fuck-buddy status.

"Hey, it's me," I said after I rang her apartment. She didn't respond, instead, the buzzer sounded and I walked inside.

"What the hell happened to you?" she said when she saw me limping up the stairs.

"You should see the other guys."

"Why were you fighting? Where's your shirt?"

"Remember when I told you I had to go help a friend? Well, helping her meant fighting off the guys that drugged her."

She took me by the hand and led me back through her living room, past the kitchen, and into the bedroom. After pushing me on the bed she said, "I'll be back in a second." She disappeared into the bathroom and came back holding a purple jar. "I've got Emu oil. I use it when my muscles get sore. It should help with all these bruises."

"How does it do with concussions?"

"I've got aspirin."

She moved me around and rubbed me down. Even if she didn't care for me in the relationship sense, she liked having sex with me. In her book, that was enough of a reason to keep me around.

"You said guys...so how many were there?"

"Five. Just some dumb-ass, college kids. Classic case of they slipped something in a girl's drink and her friend called me to help. I showed up, got her out of the house, and pointed some misplaced rage in their direction."

"Well, it looks like they pointed a car in your direction and put the hammer down," she said as she massaged the bruised ribs on my left side.

"Actually I think that one was a Berkinstock. What a fag, right?"

"You're the one that knows what a Berkinstock is."

We both laughed and I gripped my left side in agony. "Don't make me laugh. It hurts to laugh."

"Oh, pobrecito." She rubbed my head with an open hand. "And here I thought I was gonna get laid tonight. But, alas, my man is in no shape to perform."

"I knew you cared. If you take good care of me I still might be able to help you out. You'll have to be on top though. I can't get to breathing too hard."

"What would be the fun in that? I'm drunk. I wanna lay around and get some dick." She kissed my forehead, making sure she missed the big black spot on the side of my face. "I'm just glad you're okay." There was a genuine look of liking me in her eyes. I didn't have to read her mind to know that she was happy to see me whether she was getting laid or not. All in one moment I felt better, I grew to love someone new, and I started to forget about Somebody That I Used To Know. I wasn't sure how it felt for Jess, but I thought moving on felt great.

Chapter 8

The other half of the bed was empty when the sun cut between the curtains and woke Holt up. Holt had the feeling that Cat was only going to be a one night thing, so it was probably good that she left while he was still asleep. It saved them both from the awkward conversation about why she was leaving. Although Holt would have accepted an excuse like a meeting early on a Sunday morning without question, he was glad she was able to escape without having to give one.

He put on a pot of coffee when he got out of bed. By the time he finished a quick shower, the pot was finished brewing. He drank a cup while he dressed, but he was surprised when he saw a stranger standing in the mirror. The stranger had a three day beard and it looked like he had worn the same suit since Friday morning. He had waited long enough to get a haircut that the hair on the back of his head was starting to curl. Holt remained so well groomed in New York that he forgot how ruggedly handsome he looked when he let himself go a little bit. Although he liked the stubble and the longer hair, it was definitely time to get some clothes to make it through the rest of the weekend.

He started toward the door, but he needed to get a couple things together in order to fully start his day. He took a seat at the desk and went to work rolling two joints. It was only the third attempt Holt made at rolling since he resumed smoking weed two days earlier, and already he was rolling like a pro. Sure, the results were nowhere near perfect. The first joint could have been a little tighter over the length and the second one could have been a little skinnier. Even with their shortcomings, they were worthy of being called joints. He put one joint inside his cigarette pack and the other he tucked into the breast pocket of his button-up shirt.

He drove toward the Monmouth Mall, but he took an alternate route. He could have headed straight to the Parkway, but he wanted to make sure he had enough time to finish a joint before he got into Brielle. He stuck to the state roads and highways south of Interstate 195. The shore-bound traffic was more concentrated around the interstate and the Parkway, and he could enjoy his smoke along the less populated rural roads. He learned long ago that he didn't have to pay attention to where he was going when he drove through that part of New Jersey. The population distribution was pretty even across the central and southern portions of the state. The back roads were lined with trees and the occasional country home. The roads weren't empty, but traffic was light enough there was no need to worry about getting caught. He was usually lost when he finished smoking on his little adventures, but it was never too long until he found a sign to point him back in the right direction.

When he was almost finished with his joint, he rolled down the windows and made his way back toward the Parkway. He cruised north toward the mall, taking the last few puffs before throwing the roach out the window. By the time he got to the mall, he was walking on clouds. His high was probably noticeable as he crossed the parking lot toward the department store at the south end of the mall. When he got inside and began his search for men's wear, his phone rang.

"I'm sorry I missed your call last night," Alex said after Holt answered. "I was out and I didn't have my phone."

"Don't apologize. It wasn't a big deal. I was at the bar last night and Sera showed up with her boyfriend. I freaked and needed someone to calm me down."

"I'm sorry. I don't know if I could have said anything to make it better. I would have told you to go somewhere else, but I doubt you would have listened."

"You're probably right."

"What are you up to today?"

"I didn't bring a change of clothes with me when I left Friday. I'm at the store now."

"Are you buying a new suit?"

"I don't know if I have time to get something tailored before Sera's bar-be-que this afternoon."

"So buy something that doesn't need tailored. I bet you they have some really great sales on jeans and t-shirts."

"It is a little warm for a suit today." Holt had already stopped in front of the rack of jeans right off the main isle in men's wear. He dug though the rack to see if there were any in his size while he talked to Alex. "And I'm a little scruffy right now."

"That sounds pretty sexy. I think you should listen to the girl in this debate."

"I'll think about it."

"Good. When are you coming back to New York?"

"I'm definitely staying down here tonight and maybe tomorrow night. I'll call you tomorrow at some point and let you know how everything's going."

When he ended the call, he already had three pairs of jeans under his arm and he was half way to the dressing room. He tried them on to make sure they fit right before going to the underwear section to pick out a pack of black t-shirts and a cheap pack of boxers. He didn't get any socks. Instead, he grabbed a pair of flip flops. His shoes were in no shape to wear around town, and the warm air of summer was no time to wear shoes anyway.

With flip-flops, jeans, underwear, and shirts under his arm, Holt made his way toward the registers near the store entrance. It was Saturday and the lines were long. There was no real way to pass the time quickly with full hands, so he turned and stared at the rack of magazines at the end of the check-out line. It was sad to think that the highest point in journalism was no longer writing for the top tier newspapers. Although Holt never wanted to be a journalist in his writing days, he still thought the idea of a Pulitzer was as romantic in the writing world as finishing the great American Novel. But that's not what most people wanted in modern America. People were more concerned with who Kim was blowing on film and the latest in the Brangelina drama. Real news was what people read only when they became bored with the bad news in their own menial lives. In response to this dying of the news readership, most of the news reporters had to change their style to answer for the lower demand. The stories were all about what sold the most, but the writing itself was dying off.

"A Tale of Two Cities, right?"

Holt shook his head as he turned away from the magazine rack toward the small voice behind him. The woman barely stood up to Holt's chest. She was small and her skin was a deep olive. Her eyes were big and as black as her hair, cut so it barely brushed against her shoulders as her head moved.

"I'm pretty sure that's Charles Dickens tattooed on your arm. I recognize the phrase 'in short, it was a period so far like the present period' yada yada." She looked back up from Holt's exposed forearm, and her mouth opened as she smiled, revealing big, white teeth.

"I'm impressed." Holt turned his body beneath his head, putting his back to the register. "Most people only recognize 'It was the best of times, it was the worst of times'."

"I'm kind of a huge Dickens nerd. I've read all his books twice, and my PhD centers on him and the way he published. It's nice to know there are other Dickens fans out there."

"This may sound pretty weird, but I actually don't like any Victorian literature."

"How do you not love Dickens?"

"He's too long winded for my taste, and he uses too many adverbs – and too many phrases and clauses acting as adverbs. Whenever I read his writing I just want to cut it and edit it. I don't think I've ever made it through more than ten pages in any of his books – even when I was assigned to read them in college."

"If you hate Dickens so much why do you have his most famous quote tattooed on your arm? That's a little permanent."

"I never said I hated him. I just don't really like British Literature in general. I got the tattoo because I always loved this sentence and the way it connected the Victorian Era to the French Revolution. It proves the timelessness of the written word in the hands of a great writer."

"I'll let you off the hook for not loving Dickens," she said, leaning to the side, looking around Holt and smiling again as she straightened up, "but you may want to move up. The people behind us may not forgive us for holding up the line."

Holt's high made him hop when he saw the gap between him and the next person ahead of him. He stepped forward, but he only turned halfway back toward his conversation, keeping an eye pointed in each direction. "Where are you doing your PhD?" he asked when she was within arms' reach.

"Rutgers. I'm funded for two years and I may get a permanent placement after I finish. What do you do?"

"I'm a literary agent in New York."

"Huh. I would've guessed writer with all the tattoos."

"I used to write…a lot. But now I sell writers instead."

"It's a tough field." She stepped with Holt as the line moved forward, but, this time, she stepped closer when she stopped.

"It looks like we're about to get cut short for checkout." Holt said when he was second in line.

"The long wait has finally come to an end."

"I'd love to keep this conversation going. You wanna grab a cup of coffee or something, if you've got the time?"

"I can do that."

He turned and bent at the knees, extending his hand as far as he could with his merchandise under his arms. "I'm Holt."

She wrapped her hand around his and nodded her head, closing her eyes as she responded. "Cheryl."

"I'll wait at the door." Holt stepped up to the register, paid, and walked toward the exit. Awkward and high, he stared at the videos rental box by the door. Like the names in the headlines on the magazines, he didn't know very many movies on the screen. It was amazing how much overworking, drinking too much, and sleeping around detached him from the world. The titles he did recognized were all adaptations of books his office or competing agencies sold. It was his job to know his industry, but where had his attachment with humanity gone?

"You thinking about renting a movie?" Cheryl's voice pulled Holt's gaze from the movie machine.

"Just waiting. Got a little lost inside my own head."

"I'm parked out here." She motioned toward the door with her head.

"Me, too."

They parted ways so they could drop their merchandise in their cars before meeting back up in front of the coffee shop at the far end of the parking lot. The coffee shop was just as busy as the department store. They stepped into line together and continued the same dance they'd done when they met.

"What did you used to write?" she asked.

"I used to write just to keep myself busy. I'd write down whatever thoughts were running through my head. I even wrote a novel once upon a time. How about you?"

"Much the same. I never wrote a book, but I have a bunch of short stories filed away. I never had the patience to sit down and write a hundred thousand cohesive words."

"It wasn't easy."

"You ever try to get it published?"

"Didn't work out."

"Is that when you quit writing?"

"For the most part. I finally sat down and wrote something a few months back, but I don't know what to do with it at this point."

"I thought you worked in publishing. If anyone should know what to do with it, shouldn't you?"

"What can I get you today?" Holt was saved by the clerk behind the counter.

"I'll have a large, black coffee." Holt motioned for Cheryl to order.

"I'll have a small, iced, caramel macchiato."

Holt paid and they stepped over to the other end of the counter to wait with the rest of the mass of customers. When the barista called Holt's name he stepped forward and grabbed their drinks. All the seats inside were occupied, so they stepped outside onto the fenced in patio to find a seat.

"You're drinking hot coffee outside in the summertime." Cheryl said as they took their seats.

"It's the only way I drink coffee." When they were both in their seats Holt continued their conversation from inside. "You asked me if I know what to do with the book and, yes, I know exactly what to do. It's just that the story isn't that simple."

"Most writers would kill for the opportunity you have. You're perfectly placed to get a novel off the ground."

"Originally, I wrote the novel back in college. I wasn't an agent then and I didn't make it as a writer. I rewrote it as an anniversary present for my wife about six months ago, and I'm currently in the middle of a divorce."

"I guess I understand why publishing doesn't seem right to you." She twisted her face and took an awkward sip of her coffee. "I'm sorry if I just brought up a sore subject."

"Don't apologize. But...back to the lighter topics of conversation. Why did you stop writing?"

"Since I wasn't born with the skill to write a novel, I thought the best way to get better was through experience. When I finished college I tried to get a job – anything really – but there was nothing out there for recent college graduates. That's when I turned to grad school and the next thing I knew I was in the second year of my PhD. Now I'll probably live out my days as a teacher instead of writing the great American novel."

"You can't doubt yourself like that. There may come a day when you sit down and everything you've always hoped to write will just come out."

"For someone who wrote a book and works with writers I'm surprised you'd say that. You know as well as I do that's not how the writing process works. Creativity is hard work. I understand the creative process, but I can't seem to find the material to put on the page. You know what they say, 'Those that can, do. Those that can't, teach.'"

"And those that can't even teach, critique."

"At least I have a fall back plan." This time, when she sipped her coffee, she smiled. Holt could tell it had been a long time since she talked to anyone about writing, and Holt enjoyed the topic of conversation just as much as she did. "So what's this book you wrote?" she asked. "What's it called?"

"The title is Failing Aristotle: The Unstoppable Force meets the Immovable Object."

"I'll say this much, you've definitely got a good title on your hands. So what's it about?"

"I guess the main theme is the idea that there are all these accepted theories and philosophies, but no one takes the time to question them. The protagonist is a young military veteran who can't live a normal life inside the constraints of the real world, so he sets out to make his own rules. Although parts of him are formed in the image of the world around him, he spends his whole life trying to reshape parts of the world in his image."

"That actually sounds really great."

"I've always thought it would be pretty boring myself."

"At first, romanticism always sounds boring, but that's the type of writing that people find the most inspiring. Look at The Old Man and the Sea. It wasn't the story of a knight or a scholar or a genius. He was just an ordinary man from Cuba that fished for a living. More than that, Hemingway became famous with The Sun also Rises. It's the everyday story of an ex-pat writer in the 1920s and all the reasons he's impotent. Yet, that was the novel that embodied the lost generation. I think you should really look at publishing your book. Everyone's so wrapped up in the action and the suspense and the mystery that they've lost sight of the real world. I think people would be receptive to a novel like yours. Hell, I'd love to read it."

"I'd love to give you a copy but I only have one and it's not with me."

"I guess you'll have to publish it so I can read it."

"I could always let you borrow my copy. I really want to hear what you have to say." Holt felt a vibration in his pocket. He looked at the screen and saw a text from Mike. "I'm sorry, but it looks like I have to cut this a little short. I'm supposed to meet up with a friend of mine. Do you have any plans tomorrow night?"

"My classes don't start up for another two weeks, so I'm just hanging around my house until then."

"Wanna grab some drinks and talk some story? That way I can give you my book."

"Can I see your phone?" Holt handed her his phone and she went to work on the screen. When her phone vibrated in her hand she gave Holt his phone back. "I'll get a hold of you tomorrow night. Does nine sound okay?"

"It sounds great," Holt said as he stood to leave. "I know this really nice spot down by the beach."

Failing Aristotle

Bad Company

A company, always on the run. A destiny toward the rising sun. I was born into a dying breed, so the gypsy life was only natural. I bounced around a lot in the Navy – Chicago, Virginia Beach, San Diego, and Seattle – but I didn't even like to stay in an apartment for more than a few months. Although I lived in Bremerton, Washington, for four years, I still managed to live in six different places in the area. I didn't like the feeling of roots forming beneath my feet. That made it real hard when I met someone I really liked, but, without hesitation, I broke her heart and moved across the country to Washington DC.

Something happened when I got to the District. Sure, Jessica may have had some influence on my nature to run, but I felt like I'd found a city worth dying in – a city from which I could conquer the world. After three years in the district, I'd only lived in four places. I spent my freshman year of college in the dorms. I lived for a year in a loft above a garage on Nevada Avenue. Then I lived a summer in another place, but, due to the shame I still feel over the whole situation, I'm not sure if I'm ready to tell you about that just yet. After that summer I moved into my apartment in Bethesda. Hell, I'd already signed a lease to live there for a second year. I was tied down by my desire to finish college and I'd gotten pretty comfortable in the cozy one bedroom apartment above the loading dock. More than that, I only had one year of college left. I was on the home stretch. The gypsy inside me hadn't gone anywhere, but his voice was lower. Jessica wasn't the root tying me down, but her ability to piss me off was what convinced the rebellious gypsy inside me to come out of hiding. Although my nature was to run at the first sign of trouble, the gypsy mind won't run from a fight. Deserters we're called, but, by principle, we can't back down.

The restaurant industry was the perfect place for the gypsy life. It was probably the only industry on the planet as global as the military. People need to eat everywhere and restaurants in every part of the world liked a person with experience. Although I took a five year break to join the Navy, I'd worked in restaurants since I was fifteen, so I had enough experience to get a job almost anywhere I applied. There was no limit to where I could go in the English speaking world.

Failing Aristotle

I was at the bar like I spent most nights after I got off early. The bar was right next door to my old restaurant, and I was there to catch up with some friends I used to work with. In the service industry, we basically pass around money and free drinks. Most places would call it stealing, but there's a right way to do the wrong thing and then there's just doing the wrong thing. We usually only did the wrong thing when we were pissed off at our jobs. As long as inventory came out in the green, we didn't get in trouble. Yeah, it was buddy fucking, but we took care of our own. You couldn't say that about many other industries. Car manufacturers didn't get free cars. Hospital employees didn't get free health care. But people in the restaurant industry got free drinks at bars. If someone didn't like it, you could kiss our asses. We worked hard to please the world around us and that world treated us like crap. So we abused the system a little – most people would've done the same thing if given the opportunity.

The bartender poured me a round of shots off the rail but he only charged me for two. I dropped twenty bucks on the bar and put the drinks on a tray so I didn't need help carrying everything outside. It was my first round of the night, but all the servers had been at the bar for an hour already. They were a little ahead of me by the time I showed up.

"Let's see this new tattoo," Marcus said. Although he and I hadn't worked together in a few months, we did a good job of staying in touch.

As everyone reached for their glass on the tray I raised the sleeve on my shirt. I turned the scabbed, black ink toward the table. The girl on my left leaned in and read the prose. "'No man is an iland, entire of itfelf' – that doesn't sound right."

"That's because you're reading it wrong. It's the Middle English printing style. If the letter s falls at the beginning or in the middle of a word, it was printed with a long s. It only looks like an f, but it's read like an s."

"Okay, I'll give it another shot.

"'No man is an iland, intire of it selfe; every man is a peece of the Continent, a part of the maine; if a Clod bee washed away by the Sea, Europe is the lesse, as well as if a Promontorie were, as well as if a Mannor of thy friends or of thine own were; any mans death diminishes me, because I

82

am involved in Mankinde; And therefore never send to know
for whom the bell tolls; It tolls for thee.'

"That's spelled really weird."

"Because it was printed in the first half of the seventeenth century.
It's from a book by John Donne call <u>Devotions on Emergent Occasions</u>.
At the time he was in the higher echelons of the Anglican Church and
he lived at St. John's Cathedral in London. He'd just lost his daughter –
I think his wife died recently as well – and he'd come down with what
he thought would be a fatal sickness. He spent every day in bed
reflecting, and he often heard the sound of the funeral bells at the
church. At first, the sound made him dwell on his own death, which is
how the book starts. The first part is really depressing, but it really
transitions as the book goes on. He starts to write about heaven as this
library and life as a chapter of a book translated into a new and better
language by its end. It's written in twenty-three parts – that quote is the
most famous and it comes from the seventeenth meditation. He goes on
to talk about how the death of others should remind us not of our own
death, but of the life we still have left. If you sit down and read the
whole thing, it'll change your perspective on everything. It really
changed mine, and there aren't that many things in this world that have
done that."

"Where do you come across stuff like this?" the girl asked. "The
other day you were drunk going on about how you proved relativity and
gravity and now you're talking about some priest."

"First off, John Donne wasn't a priest. Protestants don't have priests.
Second, I proved relativity and came up with a theory that unifies
relativity with gravity and quantum mechanics."

"Whatever." Marcus jumped in. "She asked if you study anything
normal like the rest of us."

"Says the guy with a Masters in Philosophy. I've studied a little bit
of everything and I remember everything I read. It isn't my fault that I
think a little differently than everyone else. I just like to learn. Even
though I haven't learned anything in college, I still do everything I can
to make sure I educate myself outside of the classroom."

"I'm sure you've learned something in college." The boy on my
right hadn't said much since I arrived at the bar. He'd just finished

training at Marcus's restaurant and he was just starting to come out of his shell. "I've learned a lot since I started school."

"I spent my entire Navy career preparing for college. I think that was my biggest mistake. Most of the books they assign me to read in class I already have at home. At least it's saved me a lot at the campus bookstore." I reached for my shot glass at the center of the table. I held my glass in the air and motioned for everyone else to do the same. "This isn't appropriate bar conversation. On to better topics."

We tapped glasses and took our shots. Mine went down easy, but I picked what I drank every day. The looks on the rest of the faces at the table weren't as impressed as mine, but they were enjoyable none the less. The girl on my left looked like she just saw a ghost, and there was a good chance she thought about throwing up just after she swallowed. Marcus twisted his face and stuck out his tongue. His favorite drink was rail vodka, so he had no right to turn up his nose to cheap bourbon. The new kid coughed and scrambled for his drink to chase the shot.

"So what is real bar conversation?" Marcus began. "Should we be talking about all the girls we've balled?"

"Okay, no one uses the word 'balled' anymore. I'm just saying we should talk about anything but school and books. Everyone in this town is always trying to be the smartest person at the bar." My phone vibrated in my pocket. I leaned back in my chair so I could pull it out. "Fuck…I gotta take this."

I stood up and stepped away from the table as I answered the call. It was Jessica and I didn't like talking to her with others in earshot. "What's goin' on?"

"Can you please come help me?"

"Hi, Jessica, how are you? I haven't heard from you in over a week and it's really nice talking to you again."

"I'm sorry. I'll make sure I hit all the formalities the next time we speak, but I really need your help right now."

"Can't your boyfriend help you?"

"He's already out of town. He can't turn around and I really need a boy right now."

"What you mean to say is he's out of town and it's my turn back in the driver's seat."

"Please stop messing around, Mike. He left a couple hours ago and he can't make it back in time to help. One of the guys at this party slipped something in Claire's drink and I need help so she doesn't get raped."

"Just like a bubblehead to hide from a perfectly good fight." Her last word was enough to convince me. I knew I wasn't her roommate's favorite person, but rapists were my least favorite people. "Where are you?"

"I'll text you the address."

"Okay, I'm on my way." I ended the call and went back to the table. "Guys, I hate to shoot and run, but I've got an emergency."

"I tend to prefer it when men shoot and run." Marcus always laughed at his own jokes.

"At least I know I don't have to spend the night if I ever turn to the dark side." What can I say? I enjoyed flirting with gay men as much as they enjoyed it.

It was a few blocks back to my truck so I called Portia on the way there. I wasn't supposed to meet her for another hour, but there was no way I was going to help Jess and still make it to her place on time. "I know we were supposed to meet up in a little bit, but I kind of have an emergency. Can I get a rain check?"

"But I was really looking forward to our little, late night rendezvous. I hope everything's okay."

"I'm fine. Some girl got drugged at a party and her roommate's calling me to come bail them both out."

"Okay. I'm off this weekend, so I better hear from you. I'm already horny as it is."

"You're not the only one. We'll talk soon."

By the time the call ended I'd gotten the text from Jessica. I recognized the locale of the address, and I was pretty sure I'd been there before. At least I knew where I was going, and it wasn't that far away. Maybe I could get there, be done, and make it in time to spend the night with Portia.

I made sure to stick to the back roads. There were only a few places the cops hung out in Northwest Washington DC, and I knew all of them. I didn't avoid the cop that sat just north of 44th street on River Road. Instead, I made sure I stayed right at the speed limit as I crested the hill.

Once I got to Western I drove to 47th street and turned north into Maryland. The house was around a couple corners, but I knew I was at a party by the time I got there. There weren't too many people out front, but there was a mess of cars all over the quiet residential street. When I parked I tried calling Jessica, but, as usual, she didn't pick up. I sent her a text that I was outside while I surveyed the territory.

I walked from one side of the street to the other as I approached the house. I tried not to look too conspicuous as I looked around the house and into the back yard. It was the End Of The Summer, and it was still pretty warm outside at eleven PM. The backyard was full of smokers and the smell of weed was creeping around the side of the building. Although the majority of residents in the area didn't mind the occasional party, they hated the smell of marijuana. There was a good chance this party might get busted, so I needed to get in and out as fast as possible.

By the time I made it to the front porch, Jessica was walking out the door. "Thank God you're here," she said when we met at the front door.

"What's the story?"

"I knew something was wrong when Claire walked up to me and started speaking gibberish. Finally she started to stumble around. That's when I called you. I got her to a couch in the basement, but the guys in the house are already starting to circle."

"Why the hell did you leave her at all?" I grabbed Jess by the arm and started through the front door. We pushed our way in, but I didn't make it very far. If there's one thing I've learned about house parties in big cities, it's that there was never enough room to move around. That's why I mostly stuck with bars since I was old enough to drink legally. I was used to parties in the country where there was more than enough room for everyone to Kick It In The Sticks. It took me a minute to recognize the house through the mass of people rubbing up against each other in the small living room. It was the same house Jess and I spent an hour at the night we met, but I hadn't been back since. I tried to push my way through the party, but I wasn't sure where I was going. I leaned close to Jess. "You should probably lead the way."

She took me by the hand and shouldered her way through the sweaty crowd. I wasn't as small as her, so I had a little trouble keeping up as we moved through the mess of drunk, college kids. Every time I lost hold of her hand she stopped and raised her eyebrows, telling me to hurry up.

She pushed me in front of her when we got to the top of the stairs. When we got to the bottom, she resumed her place in front of me, leading me to the back of the basement. The basement was even more packed than the main floor because it was the house's main party space. It was hot and humid in the basement, and the only real room to move was around the beer pong table and in front of the refrigerator in the back of the room. It was the same refrigerator Jessica kissed me against for the first time, and that was where we were heading.

I saw Claire on the couch right next to the fridge. Her head was all the way back on the couch and her mouth and eyes were open. She may have known where she was, but she couldn't have moved if she objected. Jessica was right about the guys circling. There was already a guy on the couch with his arm around her. Her head moved from side to side and her mouth opened and closed as she tried to respond. All my other problems with date rape aside, I didn't understand how a man could possibly enjoy sex with a catatonic girl. I didn't like it when a conscious girl just lay there. I liked to get fucked back. Maybe they didn't know what it was like when The Sex Is Good.

"Hey, baby, it's time to go home." I didn't waste my time making sure she wasn't able to respond before I tried to pick her up. The guy next to her was probably waiting for the party to die down, talking to her so no one else would. He didn't want anyone to see him walking up the stairs with a girl that clearly wouldn't consent. Me, I didn't give a fuck. I was doing the right thing, so to hell with whatever anyone else thought, including the asshole next to her. He, however, wasn't so receptive to me reaching down to pick her up.

"She's fine man," he said, standing and putting his hand on my shoulder.

I motioned at his hand like you do when you're trying to brush the Dirt Off Your Shoulder. He let go and I went straight back to helping Claire without a word. That must've pissed him off even more. This time he grabbed and pulled hard enough to stand me up, but he ran into a problem when he tried to spin an unmovable object. I was still sober and stable, and I didn't feel like turning.

Once again, I said nothing. Instead, I put my right foot between his feet, bent my knees, and threw my weight into him. I was taller and heavier. When my shoulder hit his chest he stumbled backward and hit the refrigerator.

He righted himself and shook his head. As he started to move forward he said, "I'm gonna kick your ass."

He'd only made it through half a step when I turned and threw a punch, but I didn't aim at him. I had no intention of destroying my opponent. I only needed to destroy his willingness to engage. Instead, I put my fist into the freezer door right next to his head. The power of my punch was enough to make the whole thing tip back and rock. The room stopped at the bang.

My elbow was inches from the bridge of his nose. As I pulled my fist back from the freezer, his eyes followed the length of my arm. He probably didn't know Latin, so I'm sure he didn't understand the gravity of the quote tattooed on the outside of my forearm. 'The die is cast' was printed right in front of his eyes. Once my arm was at my side, he was left with the sight of my fist print in his freezer door. A solemn, flat expression overcame his face, and he never looked away from the dents. My action was enough to make him yield, but I wasn't so quiet.

"Touch me again and I'll break your collarbone." I put my back to him and leaned down again to help Claire. Her eyes were open and hollow. I put one of her arms around me as I got down to her level and wedged my arms underneath her. I made sure to lift with my legs and she curled up with her head on my shoulder as I stood. She mumbled something in my ear as we turned from the couch. It probably would have been 'Thank you' if she had any real motor control. I was glad I got her out of there, because she would have remembered everything if I hadn't. "She's coming with me," I said as I turned from the couch. "She'll be fine when I get her home."

The crowd got out of my way as I walked. They were probably scared I might do to them what I'd just done to the freezer. Jessica was already heading toward the stairs when I got to her. She pushed her way through the crowd and led the way up. I realized then how narrow the stairs were, and I had to be careful that I didn't hit Claire's head on the wall as I carried her.

We maneuvered through the crowd upstairs and toward the door. A few people moved out of the way when they saw Claire in my arms, but most were only aware of the party going on around them. Luckily, it was hot as hell upstairs, and the crowd had already thinned in the few minutes we were in the basement. When we got outside we practically ran to my truck.

"Where are your keys?" Jess asked when we were close.

"My right pocket I think." I stopped when we were a few steps away from the truck so she could get them. I was wrong, so I turned my other hip to her and said, "We need to hurry. Those guys aren't gonna be too happy with me."

"Maybe next time you'll remember the right pocket."

"I did remember the right pocket, just not the correct one."

"This isn't the time for jokes, Michael." Jess opened the door and I set Claire in the passenger seat, sliding her in feet first and making sure to set her head back. I looked toward the house as I buckled her seatbelt. There was already a posse coming out the front door. The kid from the basement was at the back of the pack and it looked like he recruited some bigger friends to come and have a chat. I liked chats as long as they were appropriate drinking conversation.

"Get her home safe," I said as I turned to join the boys walking off the porch and into the street.

"Where the hell are you going?" Jess grabbed me by the shoulder. When I turned and looked her mouth was open and her teeth were clenched together. She knew exactly where I was going.

"I gotta buy some time so you can get out of here. Besides, I've got some misplaced rage that needs handled."

"We've got enough time we can still get out of here."

I stepped hard enough she couldn't hold onto my shoulder anymore. "They might hurt my truck."

After ten paces or so I heard Dakota's driver door shut and the engine turned over. Jessica may not have been too happy with me but I didn't care anymore. It was Saturday night, and, last time I checked, Saturday Night's All Right For Fighting. I was only ten yards from my new friends. I stopped and let them come to me. I figured I was the center of attention at this point, so they should make the trip. I looked past them and people were pouring out the front door to watch as my truck drove off without me.

There was a big guy in the group of five heading my way. He stepped out ahead of the others and they formed a line abreast behind him. "I'm gonna take that damage out of your ass," he said as he positioned himself in front of me.

"You'll do no such thing." I looked over my shoulder. The tail lights were already gone. The die really was cast. When I looked back at him I said, "You should do what everyone else does and just sue me."

"You got a smart mouth for a dead man."

"Hate to tell you but you're gonna need a bigger army to kill me. It looks like there's plenty of people over there if you wanna recruit some more. I'll wait here." I smiled as I finished. I never smile.

"Cocky, too." The big guy said as he stepped closer. He had a few inches and maybe twenty pounds on me. There was a good chance he knew how to handle himself, but I wasn't worried. He felt comfortable in the company of a superior force, but he'd fall to his own hubris as most men in that situation did. Divide and conquer was only the appropriate stratagem if the divider knows anything about conquest.

I leaned around the big guy and pointed at the Kid from downstairs. "This little talk is gonna cost you a collarbone." As arrogant as that statement sounded, that wasn't my intention. I was a student of war long before the military. The one thing every book on warfare shared was to avoid battle at all costs. I'll admit, I could've avoided this engagement, but it was too late for that. I had to fall upon my contingencies. It was a good idea to know what I was up against before everything kicked off. I looked along the line of boys behind the big one. One kid was as tall as the guy in my face, but he was Skinny. If he got close I'd get my hands on him and shake him as hard as I could. If he didn't get close I'd just get close to him. Another guy was built like the Kid, Short and Average. The third guy was shorter, but he was stocky. He looked like a wrestler or a Rugby player. He might be a problem if he got me to the ground, so I had to keep that from happening.

I'd gotten a good look, but my observation was cut short when the big guy pushed me. He stepped up and got real close. "I'm talking to you."

"Men who like their jaws don't touch me." My heart was beating hard, so I evened my breaths to slow it down.

"What are you gonna do?" He pushed me again.

I let the force of his hands move me back until there was a close arm interval between us. I had to answer his question, but I had nothing to say to him. You see, actions speak louder than words, and an action was my answer. I exploited what tacticians refer to as the element of surprise. He made the first fatal error possible in any battle: he underestimated his enemy.

I used a trick my buddy Jason taught me to use when I was outsized. He demonstrated the move on me enough times that I couldn't help but learn it. I ran my fist up and into the big guy's neck as hard as I could. Post-impact I opened my palm, rolling it around the right side of his head. Afterward I crossed my arms – my left below my right – and gripped both sides of his head. All I had left to do was drive both my palms toward my knee as hard as possible. It was over in an instant. The sound of him hitting the ground reminded me of a slab of meat landing on a cutting board. He shook like a recently dead body. There was some wheezing, though, so I knew he was still alive. He'd damn sure remember that one when he woke up, but he wouldn't be able to tell anyone about it for at least four to six weeks. I'd crossed the first mountain on my journey, and there were only four hills left to conquer before I was home free.

I was bigger than everyone in the rest of the group, but they still had a combined weight between six hundred fifty and seven hundred pounds. But my actions gave me further advantage. The sight of the big guy half dead on the ground was enough to make their whole formation take a step back. The Small and Average kid took it a step further. First, he stumbled back. When he caught himself, he ran past me down the street. I let the coward go. There was no reason to worry about a man scared enough to run away from a fight. He'd have to live and die with the shame he brought to his family, and that was victory enough for me. Three to go.

Although the group was already smaller by nearly half, the remaining boys were smart enough to surround me. It was like an old David Karadean movie, but I wasn't a Kung Fu master. I knew I could hit harder than any of them – and they didn't look like they'd taken many hits in their day – but they still had me outnumbered. There was no good ending to this fight. All there could be was victory. I was gonna have to hurt these guys a little or they were going to seriously hurt me. The priority was keeping my composure. I closed my eyes and took a deep breath as they circled. It would take some time before they started to move in. Although they were stronger as a whole, I was stronger than any of the individual parts. I wasn't going to give them any time to confer on strategy when they were short their strongest ally. Unless they knew how to work as a cohesive unit, the advantage was in my favor. I was a caged animal, and I could see the fear growing in their eyes.

They gave me an opportunity to keep moving forward, so it was on me to capitalize on their hesitation. Skinny was standing right in front of me. His eyes were still wide from witnessing the brutal scene with his big friend, and he didn't even put his hands up as I got close. I put a straight right into his nose. He fell back a couple steps and I made sure to keep moving in that direction. Even though the decision left my back exposed, it was best to try and get him all the way out of the fight while I could. I grabbed the collar of his shirt when I hit him in hopes pulling him toward me would make the force of the hit increase. I didn't hit him in the middle of the face this time, though. I focused lower on his chin. He was as tall as me so I could hit straight and get a solid connection with his lower jaw. After I landed a couple swings, there was a hand on the collar of my shirt. One of my opponents was trying to turn me away from Skinny, but my feet didn't move. All he did successfully was tear my shirt half way down the front.

I looked and Rugby was staring back at me. I turned with all my weight and pushed Skinny toward Rugby. Although they didn't hit one another hard enough to hurt, I kept pushing them both and it was enough to make Skinny stumble and grab at Rugby for support. I pushed them to the ground and their fall gave me a minute to find and deal with the Kid. I swiveled on my feet like I was playing Bull in the Ring. It didn't take me long to find him. When I laid eyes on him he started to backpedal toward the house, but I was on top of him in two paces. I took him straight to the ground and went to work.

He tried to squirm when I mounted him, but my knee was pressed straight into his sternum, holding him in place. He put his hands up to protect his face, but that wasn't what I was after. I hammered down on his shoulder, just below his neck. When I was a kid, I blew out my right shoulder. Since then my left arm was stronger than my right. Although the left-handed punches weren't as accurate, they were much harder. With every connection, there was a thudding sound of bone against bone. With every swing, my punches got heavier and I drew back farther. My hand hurt like hell right off the bat, but the adrenaline pushed the pain to the back of my mind. I had to break him while I had the chance. When his clavicle finally gave, I'd already won enough to satisfy my rage.

He screamed. I smiled again. Only problem was that I didn't get much time to revel in the victory. A foot in the back of my ribcage knocked the wind out of me, and I rolled off the Kid. I scrambled. I had to get back to my feet. The first time I tried to get up I saw Rugby standing over me. I made it onto my hand and knees. Shortly after, I felt his foot in my ribs again. The pain of that impact shot through my chest, up my neck and out my mouth. The kick was enough to roll me over. I couldn't tell if he'd broken anything, but I needed a second before I got going again. I managed to get myself half way to my feet, but I got another kick. This time, it was a kick to the face.

That Skinny bastard put the sole of his shoe into my eye socket. At least I wasn't thinking about the sharp pain in my ribs anymore. To make matters worse, the Kid was getting his feet underneath him. It was one thing to let his friend run off, but I wasn't done punishing him yet. I had to make short work of Skinny and Rugby as they advanced. The good thing about people that have no real education in combat was that they didn't breathe very well. It's important to inhale and exhale with every movement. Most people are familiar with aerobics – repetitive physical activity based on an individual's breathing pattern. Few understand the concept of anaerobic activities like boxing and sprinting. A fighter runs his body into oxygen deprivation within the first minute of a fight. He may stay on his feet if he doesn't breathe, but he won't last long if he gets hit. Through the flurry of feet and fists, I could tell the two of them weren't breathing. I put an elbow under Rugby's ribs and followed through with a fist into the Skinny's stomach. The power of their attacks faded. Their eyes went wide. They weren't just short of breath. They couldn't breathe at all. I thanked God that rich kids never learn to fight.

It didn't take me long to get to my feet. I pushed my breathless attackers back and went straight for the Kid. He was almost upright so I pushed him back down. I wasn't going back to the ground with him, but I wasn't going to let him go anywhere either. He caught himself with both arms – even the one with the broken clavicle – and his legs were almost straight out behind him. He turned onto his side, but I couldn't tell if he was trying to crawl away or if he was trying to beg for forgiveness. I'd grant him absolution when the time came, but there's no mercy in hell, not when I'm the devil.

His leg was horizontal and fully extended. There was some space between his knee and the ground, so I did the first thing that popped into my head. I stomped down on his knee as hard as I could, and, I'll tell you this much, he was never going to dance again. I couldn't tell what was louder: the pop of his tearing MCL or the crunch of his breaking Patella. The only thing I knew was that I heard the Careless Whisper of them both. They were terrifying sounds, but the sound that came after them was even worse. The scream could've shattered glass, and it was music to my ears. I wasn't finished with him, but he was one step farther down the path to righteousness.

The scream was enough to stop his friends in their places. They were both on their hands and knees trying to get back to their feet after almost passing out from a lack of oxygen, but they were in momentary shock. I wheeled the tip of my steel-toed boot right into the bridge of the Skinny bastard's nose. What followed looked like something out of an old boxing movie. His whiplashing face let loose a stream of blood and spit as the force of my foot flipped him onto his back. Although my kick to his face was more effective, I considered the two of us even.

As I watched Skinny hit the ground, I smiled wide and forced my eyes open so far it hurt. I didn't want to risk missing anything. The justified violence was more fun than the kinkiest sex, and the pain that came with it made me feel more alive than the truest love. I stayed to fight because I wanted to feel something for the first time in a long time, but the only thing I felt was unadulterated joy brought on by letting loose to Break Stuff. I didn't even feel the rugby kid's shoulder in my side when he tried to tackle me. I just laughed at the fact he repeated an earlier mistake, trying to move the immovable. I wrapped my arms around his waist and lifted him over my shoulder. It was the first time in my life I'd ever powerbombed someone. I didn't feel bad or anything, but I was lucky I didn't kill him.

The Kid was on his back, dragging himself away with his good elbow. After I walked up and kneeled down beside him, I grabbed his shirt with both hands and sat him up.

"Do you know why I stayed behind?" I asked through bloody lips and teeth.

"Because you're a fucking psycho."

I laid him back down and put one hand over his nose and mouth. I used the heel of my other palm to rest my weight on his broken clavicle, and I felt bone grinding on broken bone beneath my hand. He struggled with his good hand, but it was no use. When I saw the tears in his eyes I let him go.

"I stayed to punish you for what you were going to do to that girl. Look at what you did to your friends." I turned his face so he had to look at his allies beaten and bloodied in the street. Whenever he tried to close his eyes to hide his mind from the scene, I forced his eyelids up. "Now, you're going to confess. Or you'll die." I pointed toward the crowd near the house. "They won't do anything to protect you. They won't even call the cops because they don't want to get in trouble for the drugs and drinking. It's just you and me now."

"Fuck you."

Again, I put my hand over his nose and mouth, pushing the bridge of his nose and his jaw toward one another. With the entrance to his airways blocked, I gripped his throat hard with my free hand and set all my weight on his chest. I leaned in close to his ear and whispered, "You can stay quiet. I think I'll enjoy the sight of the life leaving your eyes more than the sound of your confession."

He struggled below my weight, but the lack of oxygen slowed him down. His eyes blinked slower and slower as his struggles became softer and softer. I felt the very moment he gave in, but I held on a little longer. I've looked into the mouth of death several times, and the first time was by far the most terrifying. It's not the thought of impending death, but, instead, the fear of death's pain that struck the heart hardest. If I was going to change this Kid through punishment, I had to push him to death's doorstep before I gave him absolution. His mouth moved beneath my palm, trying to make words as his eyes rolled back. I took him to the point when the pupils dilate and everything gets bright and quiet.

I pulled my hands away from his airway and lifted my weight off his chest. "What do you have to say?"

"I drugged her."

"What were you gonna do after."

"I was gonna take her to my room," his voice dropped as he spoke, "and take advantage of her."

"You were gonna rape her."

"Yes."

"Say it."

Tears fell from the corners of his eyes and his voice was broken by quiet crying gasps. "I was gonna rape her."

"Louder. I want them to hear it," I said as I put my hand back around his throat and pointed to the crowd.

He screamed it. Every eye in the crowd went saucer shaped. After a couple of seconds staring the crowd started to break. No one went back inside the house. Instead the bystanders started walking toward cars and down the street. No one wanted to party with an admitted rapist. I stood to follow suit, but, before I walked away, I said to the Kid, "I forgive you."

He'd never make that mistake again. Sometimes the only way to cure a man of sickness was pain, not isolation. If justice had any idea of what was and wasn't just, prisons would cure criminals of criminal intent instead of breeding more, better criminals. I, a simple military veteran, cured the worst kind of criminal of his desire to rape a woman by showing what the will of the righteous was capable of.

As I turned to leave, I caught sight of a man standing in his front yard. He couldn't have been that much older than me, but his bath robe and minivan told me he had a family. He had a cordless phone in his hand, and he ended a call as I turned and faced him.

"What that kid just said, was that true?" he asked.

"Every word."

"I called the cops. They'll be here any minute." He opened the gate to his fenced in property. "There's an alley behind my house. You can cut through my yard. I didn't see where you went."

I lowered my eyes to the ground in submission. I made sure to thank him before he disappeared inside his house, but I said nothing else as I passed through the yard. The path of righteousness had its perks, but I didn't want to ruin the favor that man did for me.

Although I may have been one of the righteous, that didn't stop the adrenaline from fading. When it did, the sore spots all across my body came to life. My swollen left hand started to throb while my face and side felt like a dance floor. I may have only been on the ground for a few seconds, but that was more than enough time for them to do some damage. Luckily, I had a pretty thick skull. All I needed to make myself feel better was a stiff drink.

Chapter 9

A plume of smoke rolled out the door as Holt stepped out of his car. He thought about the last time he hot boxed a car, but the memory evaded him. It was definitely before he and Sera moved to New York, but he had no idea whether it was in his Dakota or Mike's Jeep Wrangler. Either way he missed the feeling of doing something wrong. He lived such a legally obedient life in New York, the land of delivery weed, but he felt like an outlaw once again. Getting high did not mean he was hurting anyone, although getting high while driving around the busy, cop ridden Jersey Shore in the middle of summer was probably not the smartest idea. Fuck it. He was dressed in jeans, a t-shirt, and flip-flops for the first time in over a half a decade. It was okay to be a rebel again.

"Do you have any cologne?" Mike asked as he stepped out of the car. "I don't want to walk inside smelling like weed."

Holt stopped halfway around the back of his car and looked at Mike. Holt scrunched his face and said, "Riddle me this Batman: I quit smoking weed like five years ago and I just started up again two days ago."

"What's your point?"

"You've been smoking weed almost every day since you got out of the Navy, right?"

"It was like a year after I got out before I started smoking again."

"I don't understand why you're the paranoid one in this situation."

"Because your father-in-law's a cop and I don't feel like going to jail. You know how much I hate being away from my kids."

"He's retired…he doesn't care anymore. Besides, cops don't like to shit where they live. The last thing a cop wants is the police ruining a good time. Pull out your tampon and come inside. The twins'll be here any minute, I'm sure."

Holt led the way up the driveway and past the blue Chevy Silverado that filled the space between the garage and the side of the house. It would have been easier to cut through the house, but they were both narrow enough to squeeze between the truck and the garage. When they slipped through the gate into the back yard Holt's high finally hit him. He smiled wide as he waved at Sera and the man she was at the bar with the night before. They were both up on the deck by the grill, and they looked like they were having words. Sera left the conversation to meet Holt and Mike by the gate.

"Last night I figured you'd called off your date with Mike. I figured you show up with that girl in red."

Holt wrapped his arms around Sera as he said, "Although it kills me to see you with a new man, I wouldn't do that to you."

"I see." Sera only half returned his hug before stepping past Holt to give Mike a real one. "When is Cait coming by? I haven't seen the twins in days."

"I texted her a few minutes ago, but she hasn't gotten back to me."

"She's like that sometimes."

Mike pulled out his phone to text his wife again and the three of them walked up to the deck together. Sera walked back to her boyfriend by the grill while Holt and Mike took a seat at the big white deck table with the old man sitting by himself in silence. Holt looked sideways at the manuscript in the old man's hands.

"Good to see you again, Phil. I see you got your hands on my book."

"I'll never understand why you wrote about a military veteran when you never actually served in the military." Phil never looked away from the book as he spoke.

"That's how fiction works. The narrator is not necessarily the book's author. I actually based the character off Mike."

"Well I could have guessed that by how much marijuana the guy smokes." Phil looked over the rim of his glasses at Mike. Mike's eyes grew as he took his seat. He looked down at his phone trying to ignore the comment.

"What do you think so far?"

"It took me a couple chapters to realize the story is in reverse. It's not too bad though. If you let me finish I'll tell you all you want to hear."

"I like the sound of that." Holt stood up and walked past the couple by the grill. Matt was having trouble getting the grill to light, and Sera was getting hungry. She got grumpy when she was hungry. It did not take a clairvoyant to see she was agitated. Without a word, he stepped into the house.

Once he was through the kitchen he stopped at the bottom of the stairs. Normally Holt would have used the downstairs bathroom, but he decided to take a trip down memory lane. He looked over his shoulder before running up the stairs. At the top he looked left into Sera's room. The last time he was in her room was a little hazy. It must have been just before they moved to New York. The first time he saw her room, however, was a crystal clear memory. It was just before he moved to Colorado. He drove up to New Jersey just after graduation. Sera was home for the summer, and he was still trying to convince her to come with him. Her dad was gone and they spent the day abusing every piece of furniture in her room except the dresser. It looked the same as it did a decade earlier. Her desk was still right below the single, two-pane window opposite the door. Her bed was still in the near corner under the pitched ceiling. Clothes were still scattered across the floor starting at a pile by the closet and spreading out the farther the pile stretched from the closet door. It looked like Sera had never moved out of the room, like she never moved to Colorado, like she never spent a day of her life with Holt.

After Holt was finished in the bathroom he rounded the corner at the top of the stairs to make it back down before anyone knew he was snooping around Sera's space. He stopped when he saw his wife sitting on her bed. He knocked on her door, but he remained on the far side of the threshold. He leaned on the doorframe as she turned to look at him.

"What are you doing up here?" she asked.

"The bathroom downstairs was occupied."

"Liar." She moved over on the bed and patted the spot next to her.

"Thank you for waiting to sign everything," he said as he took a seat beside her. "I don't think I'm ready to be divorced yet. I just want to make sure we don't hate each other before we finalize this whole mess."

"I never wanted it to come this far, believe me. Between you and Matt I didn't feel like I had a choice."

"What does he have to do with this?"

"I told him I wasn't going to move away with him while I was still married to you. He knew I had divorce papers. I just hadn't signed them or given them to you. He practically made me send them."

"He doesn't know you're having second thoughts."

Her bottom lip shook a time or two and her eyes glossed over as she nodded. "Fuck you and your…telepathy."

"I didn't have to read your mind to know that. I've had that feeling since you called me Friday night." And after everything she said at the sea wall.

Sera's eyes were still moist as she turned to look at him, but tears never fell. "Bullshit. I'm not gonna say you're lying, but I know you're not being completely honest."

"Who's telepathic now? All I'm going to say is this: I know I screwed up. I know this is my fault, but you always have a choice. I would never say no if you came back to me. I didn't bring a date today because I'm not going to rub another woman in your face, even if it kills me to see you with Matt."

"Then what was last night all about?" Her eyes dried instantly, and her face pointed. She had that narrowed look that cut right through Holt's fearless exterior. It took every ounce of his strength to keep his hands from shaking.

"I got territorial and a pretty girl sat down next to me. I would have been a fool to say no to her."

"Stop making excuses. You were drunk and being an asshole. You knew I was there and you knew what you were doing. You seem to forget that Mike tells Cait everything, and she and I have a tendency to share some things, too. Your inability to say no is half the reason I had no choice. I tried to come back to you once, but you were occupied. So I left again."

She stood and started walking back toward the stairs. Holt watched her as she passed and stood to follow.

"Is that when you took my bag and the rings and the envelope and the picture?" He stepped quickly as she flew down the stairs. "I know you took the envelope to give it to Mike, but why didn't you take the picture the night you left." He nearly had to run to keep up with her after she turned the corner at the bottom of the stairs. "But why the backpack? You could have fit everything in that big ass purse of yours."

She walked back outside to rejoin her boyfriend by the grill. "You still haven't started the grill yet?" she asked.

Holt continued past the couple. He looked to the big white table. Mike had sunk down into his chair because Phil was staring at him over

101

the book. Mike kept his eyes on his phone as best he could, but he couldn't help but stare back at Phil through his brow every once in a while.

"Phil, be nice to Mike. He gets paranoid when people stare at him. Even more so when people stare at him while he's high. I made him do whatever we did on the way over here. It isn't his fault if he's forced."

"But it's so much fun to watch him squirm." Phil smiled for the first time as he looked back down at the book. Holt could see that he was getting close to the end already.

"You scare me, Phil," Mike said as he sat up a little higher in his chair.

Phil's eyes narrowed as he glared back at Mike. Mike sank back into his chair and Holt laughed out loud. "Mike, I used to be over here all of the time. He and I have had this discussion. You can relax." Holt grabbed a chair and took a seat next to Phil. He shifted the chair closer and he looked to make sure that Sera was still focused on yelling at her boyfriend.

"Phil, I need to ask you something."

"I'm trying to read. I'd love to tell you what I think of your book before you leave town. If you don't give me a chance to finish I don't get the chance to tell you what I think."

"This will only take a second."

"If I answer your question you can't interrupt me anymore."

"It's questions actually, but you've got a deal." Holt waited for Phil to close the book, holding his place with his finger as he set the book in his lap.

"Do you know anything about Sera trying to come back to me?"

"I think my kids are here," Mike said as he stood to leave.

"C'mon Phil. I know you know something."

"All I know is that one morning she went to New York to talk things out with you. I assumed everything worked out because she didn't come home that night. The next morning she showed up in the same clothes she was wearing when she left smelling like a three day bender."

"When did this happen?"

"Back in January. Right after she first came down here."

"Do you know where she went?"

"Couldn't tell you."

"She never told you what happened?"

"She had you're old backpack in one hand and divorce papers in the other." Phil reopened the book and went back to reading. "I didn't ask."

"Why didn't she send the divorce papers then?"

Phil kept his eyes down and pursed his lips as he read.

"You've gotta know something."

Phil shrugged his shoulders and Holt shifted his attention to the escalating conversation taking place by the grill. He had been at the house for almost thirty minutes and the grill was still cold. Holt went over to handle the situation before it led to a break up.

"Mind if I give it a shot?" Holt asked when he got close. "The igniter is busted. This isn't the first time I've had this problem with the grill." Holt reached down and opened the gas valve all the way. Gas hissed as Holt used his lighter to get a piece of paper going. "The trick is to throw a match or something down into the gas and hope you don't blow up the house or singe your eyebrows."

Matt walked away at the sound of the grill lighting. Holt closed the lid and grabbed a hand full of beers out of the cooler. He handed two to Sera. "Go inside and relax. You two spent the whole day getting everything ready. I can run the grill. It'll be like old times...sort of."

As he waited for the grill to heat up, he heard the sounds of salutations and kids inside the house. He walked to the back door and watched through the glass. Mike and Cait were standing at the mouth of the hallway with the twins. Mike was setting his little girl on the floor and Sera bent down to give her a hug. Cait had both her hands on her son's shoulders trying to hold him in place. Although the twins were very well behaved, they knew what it meant when they came over to Sera's for a bar-be-que – infinite playtime for the afternoon. The hyperactivity was growing in their eyes every second. Holt smiled and stepped through the door making sure to slam it and get the kids' attention.

"Uncle Holt," the girl screamed as she ran from her father to the back door where Holt squatted to meet her. The little boy was right behind her.

"You two got big," Holt said as he grabbed a kid in each arm. It had been six months since he laid eyes on the twins. He had a little trouble when he scooped them up and carried them to the kitchen counter. He set them on the island in the middle of the kitchen, one beside the other so he could look them both over. They shared their parents' matching hazel eyes, but they had their mother's smooth, clear skin. They were built like their father – tall for their seven years and skinny as a flag pole. "It's been a long time. Do you two even remember me?"

"Yes," they said in unison.

"You're Uncle Holt," the little boy said. "Mommy told us you were coming today." He wrapped two skinny arms around Holt's neck. "I missed you."

"I missed you, too. I don't even know if I remember your names." He looked at the little girl. "Your name is…?"

"Her name's Taylor, silly," her brother shouted, always protective with his nine and a half minutes of seniority.

"Taylor. Oh, man, I can't believe I forgot that. It has been a long time." He stepped to his left toward the little boy. "And your name is…Ford, right? You look like a Ford."

"No!" the twins screamed together.

"Chevy?"

"No!"

"I thought it was a type of truck, but those are bad trucks." Holt tapped his chin and smiled like he was having trouble remembering. Enthralled with the two little ones he missed so much, he forgot that other people were in the room. Cait, Mike, and Matt were making their way out the back door and Mike went straight for the cooler. Sera, however, was leaning against the refrigerator near the hallway that led to the living room and the stairs. Holt looked at her as he pondered the possibility of names, and smiled at the woman he missed calling his wife. "I think I remember," he continued, looking back at the twins, "it's Dakota. Like my old truck."

"Yeah!"

He hugged them both and lowered them off the counter to the floor. "Let's get you down before Phil sees you up there and yells at me."

The kids ran outside. Holt watched through the window as the twins attacked Phil in his chair. They jumped into Phil's lap and he wrapped his arms around them, working hard to keep his place in the book. Each one sat on a different leg and they laid their long bodies over his large stomach. When Holt turned to walk back outside he was startled by Sera standing in his way. She had moved from her spot by the fridge to Holt's side, watching the twins with her father.

"They really did miss you. Every time I watched them since I moved down here they asked about you. You're really good with them."

"I missed them, too. And I like to think their just good with me. I play along. I'm still a kid myself, you know."

Sera turned to walk outside and Holt followed. Holt stayed up by the grill while everyone sat at the big round table. Phil started reading out loud to the children and the others at the table sat in silence. The grill was hot enough Holt started to cook. He stood by himself as the two couples, the old man, and the twins had story time. Holt listened to Phil read in between the hisses of meat on the grill. Phil was past the drunken, angry, vulgar beginning and he was well into the happier end – the story Holt wished he could have lived with his wife in college and how he dreamed he could have met her and fallen in love with her. Although the story was much more laid back in the last few chapters, there were still moments in which Phil had to stop reading out loud to protect the young, virgin ears of the children in his lap. Taylor was half asleep against Phil's big, warm belly, but Dakota was enthralled with the story of Mike and Jessica.

After Holt pulled the hot dogs off the grill and put the cheese on half the burgers, he walked over to the table. "Food's almost ready. Come get it while it's hot."

"You're not gonna make our plates?" Cait asked.

"Why not take our orders and bring it all to us?" Sera joked.

"I like their plan." Mike said as he stood to get some plates ready.

Instead of walking to the grill, Matt went to the cooler. Holt was afraid his presence was pushing Matt to the periphery of the group. Although Holt hated the idea that Matt was sleeping with Sera, he was trying to accept all the reasons why that was the case. Holt walked over to the cooler and extended his hand. "I don't think I've properly introduced myself. Sera's manners are a little lacking sometimes. I'm Holt."

"I know who you are. I know why you're here."

"I'm here to sign my divorce papers and get Sera's help selling my apartment. I'll be out of the way soon enough. I had my chance with her and I wasted it. You have nothing to worry about."

"What makes you think I'm worried?"

"You're crushing beers like it's your birthday, brother."

"And you're some kind of mind reader."

"I just don't want you to feel out of place here. If anyone should it's me."

"I'm sorry," Matt wiped his hand on a paper towel and returned Holt's gesture. "Here you are trying to be nice and I'm being a dick. I'm Matt."

Holt grabbed a beer and put his back to the rest of the group. "I do have to say one thing: don't break her heart, please. I did that enough for both of us."

"It's not her heart I'm worried about." Matt gave him a long look as he stepped past Holt toward the grill.

Holt stayed near the grill by himself drinking beer and eating hot dogs. Mike and Sera made plates for Phil, Cait, and the twins. Holt smiled when the group sat down to eat and the crowd went silent, the ultimate compliment for any cook. The party continued through the afternoon at the white table. Holt killed the grill when the food was no longer the center of interest. He covered the leftovers, but left them in the yard for the occasional drunk forager trying to combat the high volume drinking taking place. Oddly enough, Mike, the ex-sailor, was the only one not drinking. He had a couple beers when the party started, but, when he was finished eating, he left the group to enjoy some time with his kids. Mike may have been their father, but he was no more mature than the two seven year olds playing pretend in the backyard. His imagination was just as active as theirs, and he started a mini battle with water guns.

The conversation at the table shifted to a more adult nature in absence of the kids, but every story somehow shifted to the topic of the twins. No matter if they were talking about drinking in college or things they should have avoided in their youth, they somehow always seemed to talk about the twins in envy of the life those two still had ahead of them. Cait was sure her son would turn into a crazy asshole like his father, and Holt was sure little Taylor would be a heartbreaker at far too young an age. Phil was the only person at the table that stayed out of the conversation. He sat, flipping page after page and giving Holt dirty looks – most likely at every reference to his daughter's naked body.

Holt could not help it when he wrote the novel. He dreamed of what she would look like naked from the first time he saw her, and it was almost like a dream when he finally got the view.

As the sunlight started to fade, Phil finally closed the book and stood up, leaving the manuscript on the table as he walked inside. Holt got up and joined Matt and Cait by the grill. He chowed down a bun-less hot dog as he started to clean up the leftover food. As he cleaned, he overheard Matt telling Cait about his new job in Florida, the house he had looked at when he was down there a month before, and his plans of when and how he planned on moving. A knot made its way into Holt's throat when Matt made a comment about taking Sera with him. Holt picked up as many plates as he could carry. He needed to get away from what he heard as quickly as possible.

Mike made his way through the kitchen with Dakota asleep in his arms and Taylor following right behind him. "We're taking off. Call me tomorrow."

Matt shook Holt's hand and said goodbye as he passed through the kitchen with Sera. Holt was happy that she was nice enough to kiss Matt goodbye outside. Holt kept cleaning alone until Cait came inside and stood next to him. "I've got this," he told her.

"I'm not going to help. I came to ask about the book." She crossed her arms and leaned against the kitchen counter facing Holt. "Where's my half."

"I told you. I rewrote <u>Failing Aristotle</u> from memory. I didn't write your half so I couldn't rewrite it."

"You know how much that story meant to me."

"I know. I wish I could have done more with it when I moved to Colorado. It didn't work out."

"You can't publish <u>Failing Aristotle</u> by itself. It won't be the same."

"I know. I'm working on it."

"I still have my copy. You know people in publishing so why don't you publish it?"

"I'm taking the next week off. When I get back to work I'll see what I can do."

"Let's start getting ready." Sera had been standing behind Holt and Cait in the kitchen. She grabbed Cait by the arm and pulled her toward the stairs.

Holt used his forearm to wipe away the sheen of sweat on his brow. "Thank you, Sera," he said to himself after the ladies were gone.

"You don't have to clean up," Phil said as he joined Holt in the kitchen. "This is my house and you did all the cooking." Phil tried to step in between Holt and the sink.

"How 'bout you grab us a couple beers and you dry while I wash. I hate putting dishes away."

As Phil stepped back outside, Sera walked back into the kitchen. "Can we talk?" she asked.

"Of course." Holt looked outside at Phil. He had resumed his seat at the table where he left the book. He was sipping a beer watching Holt and Sera through the window.

Holt turned away from the sink toward Sera. "You and Cait having a girls' night?"

"Yeah. We haven't gone out in a while. Not since the beginning of summer. She's been so busy with the bar, and I've...been doing a lot less than I would like."

"Matt not entertaining you?"

"I guess I'm still getting used to him, but that's not what I wanted to talk about. Do you have any plans for tomorrow?"

"I'm grabbing drinks with a friend tomorrow night, but I don't have anything going on during the day."

"We should spend some time together."

"We should. It's been a long time since we've really hung out. I even have an idea of what we could do."

"What do you have in mind?"

"An adventure."

"Where are we going?"

"It's a surprise."

"Tell me."

"Not a chance. I seem to remember you liking surprises when we met."

"You're immovable when it comes to getting what you want." She looked at the floor. "I've missed you, Holt." She crossed her arms and look back up at him. "Although I'm still pissed at you, it was still really good seeing you today."

"I missed you, too. Let's spend tomorrow together, sign the papers, and get through the next five days. Then we can get on with the rest of our lives."

"That's fair." She stepped toward Holt and gave him a long hug. "Do I have to be up early?" she asked as she held him tight.

"Yes, but you can sleep in the car. I'll drive."

Shortly after Sera went back upstairs, Phil was back in the door with a couple beers. He started putting away the dishes that Holt had already finished washing, but he said nothing until Holt returned to the sink and started washing dishes again.

"What's with the title?" Phil asked. "How did Aristotle fail?"

"Aristotle didn't fail at anything. I consider him the first literary theorist. He wrote this book called Poetics in which he outlines his three unities: unity of time, unity of character, and unity of action. The story should be as short as possible. There shouldn't be any more characters than absolutely necessary. And the plot should be composed of sequential action. They're the basic, formalist rules of writing stories."

"You definitely broke all the rules. You started at the end of the story. There are a bunch of different characters. And the plot runs backwards. I guess you were the one that failed at Aristotle."

"You're exactly right. I wasn't trying to say that Aristotle was wrong about anything he wrote about in Poetics. The idea was that rules are meant to be broken. A good writer can follow these rules of literature outlined by Aristotle and other literary theorists, but a great writer can bend or even break the rules if they take the time to try."

The last of the dishes were dry and the food was securely stored in the refrigerator, so Holt motioned for Phil to follow him outside. By the time they finished cleaning up the afternoon's festivities, the sun was down and the night air had grown salty and cool. Holt led Phil back to the deck table and lit a cigarette as he took a seat.

"I wish I would have known about that Aristotelian stuff while I read your novel. The title makes more sense now. You always have this way of teaching people things when you speak. Even though you stick to topics for the highly educated, you have a way to keep everything understandable and at ground level. You need to find a way to do that with your novel. It's clearly a novel for the common man. Academics and literary theorists may catch on right away, but the unities are going to fly right over the head of any normal people who read it. If you're trying to write to them, you need to keep them in mind when you write."

"I had that base covered when I wrote it before, but I screwed all that up. That's why your daughter is divorcing me."

"I think her sending those divorce papers may have been the best thing that ever happened to you. This is the most dressed down I've seen you in years. You're starting to look less like a business man and more like a writer every day. Sera noticed. I could see it in her eyes."

"There's only one problem with that: we're getting divorced. I'd go after her, but I don't deserve her anymore."

"You know, if my Wanda were still alive," he crossed himself, "there isn't a goddamn thing on this planet that would keep me from coming after her."

"You don't know how bad I fucked up."

"You presume too much. There's never such a thing as messing up so bad there's no going back. You just have to be willing to tear open those fears that hold you back. You have to change yourself to change her mind. You've taken the first step by coming down here. Now you just need to follow through. She's living and happy with Matt – I'll admit it. But she was alive with you. There's a big difference between the two. The first time you and I met I was terrified of the fact that my daughter was seeing some tattooed rebel. I was sure you were going to break her heart. But that all changed when I asked you about your intentions with my daughter. Do you remember what you said to me?"

"I said 'I intend to be buried next to her.'"

"I have faith in you, Holt, and I know you're a better man than you think yourself to be. Did you make plans with Sera for tomorrow?"

"We're getting together in the morning, but you should know by now that I usually make everything up as I go." Holt put his cigarette out on his foot.

"I just don't want you to bring her back too early. You two should talk."

"I can't stay too late. I have plans tomorrow night."

"Hot date?"

"Just drinks with a Doctoral candidate from Rutgers. She wants to talk about my book, and I want to talk more about her PhD research."

"No date tonight?"

"No. I'm gonna head back to the hotel and try to write something. I miss writing." Holt began the walk toward the gate.

"That's funny. I thought you hated sleeping alone...nightmares and all." Phil stood and walked toward the house. "What did you used to call that, chasing angels?"

Holt paused before stepping through the gate. He looked back over his shoulder. "Only problem is that angels are coming up short these days...too short."

"Maybe you're looking for the wrong angel."

Waiting In Vain

From the very first time I set my eyes on her, my heart said follow through. For some reason, I had an impossible time listening to my heart. When Jess and I were together it was a roller coaster of on again off again. The worst part of the whole situation was the fact that the Merry Go Round relationship didn't stop with the breakups. Every day one of us stopped loving the other and the other started back up again. I'd like to say it was mostly my fault, but, the truth is, it was entirely my fault. That's how we wound up where we were. I had a nasty habit of breaking up with her on a daily basis. Once we were apart, she never Let Me Go. I kept pushing her away and she kept pulling me back in – even after she started dating someone else.

We were both having a hard time with the idea of being just friends, but her new relationship made it that much harder on both of us. Neither of us wanted to move on and leave the past behind us because we knew that it wasn't over between us – not by a long shot. But that didn't change the fact that I wanted a chance to be happy. She was taking a chance with someone else, and I promised to wait for her while she took that chance. She never even had the common decency to tell me when she started dating him. Obviously I knew. She didn't do a very good job of hiding it. How fucked up was it that I had to learn about her new boyfriend from Facebook. C'mon. The worst part was the fact that I had no control over what information popped up in my newsfeed, and one post brought my wait to a screeching halt.

Her boyfriend was in the Navy. They made it official when she went to Florida in March, and he deployed a week later. It was July already and his deployment was over. The post said that he was coming to see her in a few days. It wasn't the fact that she was moving on with someone new that bothered me. Over the previous year, getting her back had taken a backseat to maintaining our friendship. I was, however, extremely bothered by the fact that she was seeing this guy and I didn't have any real control over whether or not I had to hear about it. I was getting online to start some music so I had something to listen to while I wrote. His post was at the top of my newsfeed when I opened up my browser. I wasn't looking for it – I learned my lesson about Facebook stalking Jessica – but the information forced its way into my world. I didn't feel like I had a choice anymore. I deleted her from my Facebook friend's list and put the book I wrote for her in the bottom drawer of my file cabinet. I needed to get Jessica out of my head for a while, so I left my phone at home and went to a bar. It was the perfect night to Use Somebody.

A man needs a lot of confidence if he intends to walk into a bar alone and leave with a real woman. I made sure to keep my head up, my shoulders back, and my eyes forward. I walked straight through the middle of the crowd to make sure I wouldn't go unnoticed. I was always careful not to look at anyone, and I did my best to keep track of everyone that looked at me. The only girl I caught looking was the redhead at the edge of the dance floor. I was too far away to tell exactly what color her eyes were, but they were big and round and light enough that they could only be green or grey. She had a button nose, big lips, high cheekbones, and a sharply tapered jaw ending with a round chin. Although I could only see her from the waist up, the way she gripped the ledge and leaned back as she danced made me jealous of the people behind her. I was a little worried that I didn't turn more heads, but the one head I did manage to turn was one hell of a confidence boost.

I ordered a drink and posted up by the bar. It was important to be visible while staying out of the way. I wanted to make sure I had a little time to look over the bar before I made any moves. The bar was lined with people waiting on drinks, but I knew the staff. The bartender reached past all the other guests to make sure I had a drink in my hand. I turned away from the bar, leaning back on my elbows. I wasn't leaving my prime position close to the alcohol with a view of everything, and I wanted to make sure everyone around me knew it.

It was easiest to meet a girl at a bar if I took the time to get to know who was there and what they were looking for. But, even if a girl came to the bar with every intention to get laid that night, it wasn't as simple as 'nice shoes wanna fuck.' If it was that simple, I knew I was either staring down the barrel of baggage or risking my perfect STD record [Knocks on wooden writing desk just to be safe]. Usually one out of every four girls was out to meet somebody, but only about one in ten single girls at a bar will go home with someone the night they meet them. Although I had to step up to the plate and strike out a couple times if I ever wanted to be successful, I didn't have to dive in unprepared.

Unless a girl approached me, I avoided girls in groups of two or three. That was all I had to choose from along the bar, so I turned my attention to the dance floor. The dance floor was a great place to meet girls when I was in a group, but it was a totally different story when I was alone. It was never a good idea to be the lone wolf on the dance floor, so I kept an eye on things from the bar. Along the edge there were a couple guys and girls bouncing their hips like they were trying to have fun, but none were enjoying themselves enough to smile. Then there were the couples in the middle of the floor dancing like they didn't have a worry in the world. At the far end of the dance floor there was a group of at least five girls dancing in the corner along the rail. Most of the girls looked plenty good enough to go home with, but the blond dancing against the rail was the highest prospect. She was at the far side of group with her back to the dance floor. She stood up straight and ran both her hands through her hair, shaking her hips and turning around. Our eyes met from across the bar and I realized it was the redhead that checked me out when I first walked in. Her hair was bleached blond by the low light of the dance floor, an optical illusion of divine proportions. The best part of the whole situation was the two over-dressed, gelled-up, pretty boys making their way toward the redhead and her friends. My opportunity was close, but I had to time everything perfectly.

When I was alone, there was an art to getting to girls on the dance floor. Like wolves hunting, the idea was to scatter the herd and isolate the one I wanted. I never did the actual scattering, so there was always a chance I wouldn't get my opportunity. I had to wait for another guy to get in the middle of the group and scare the rest of the girls off. The girl with the biggest daddy issues usually stayed for the attention, and I had an opportunity to talk to one of the more interesting girls as the rest ran away. The main thing to keep in mind was that I couldn't be afraid to get turned down or go home alone. In my book, getting a number from an interesting girl was better than going home with a girl that's just going to lay there. Moreover, the girls I go after aren't the type to fuck someone just because they're drunk. These are the girls that only have sex with the guys they truly find intriguing. The redhead didn't find the two guys stepping in between her and her friends interesting at all. She rolled her eyes and pushed between them toward the center of the dance floor.

She saw me coming when I stepped onto the dance floor. Her eyes met mine and I made sure not to look away. She held the gaze for a minute and then she went back to dancing like she was the only person in the room. I took one more long drink to make sure my beer was empty before I got to her. I'd say what I had to say and walk away before she had a chance to respond. The idea was to confuse her, put her on her toes and keep her guessing. It left the dialogue open and removed the option of a direct rejection, perfect for all parties involved.

I leaned in close, touching her shoulder and whispering in her ear, "I really wanna dance with you, but I gotta grab a fresh beer. Don't go anywhere."

I tried to bolt before she had the chance to do anything, but she wasn't having it. She grabbed me and turned me back around. When I was facing her, she hit me on the shoulder, "Fuck that. You're going to dance with me right now and we'll go grab a drink together in a minute."

"I don't even know you and you hit me." I stepped in.

Her eyebrows went up. "And?"

I put my arm around the small of her back and pulled her close. "I think I like you already."

She smiled before she turned around. Once her back was against me she leaned her head onto my shoulder with her temple against my chin. I hooked a finger into her belt loop so I could feel the rhythm as she moved. Her shoulders didn't move from my chest and her head never left my cheek, but I'll be damned if her hips weren't moving two feet with every swing. I tried to keep up, but keeping up was damn near impossible when I was Hypnotized. Every time I moved my hips with hers she changed direction. Whenever I followed suit she moved faster. She wasn't going to make it easy on me. She had a body she knew how to use, so I had to take Control if I was going to get ahead.

I took her wrist in one hand, pressing her palm to my thigh. My other hand gripped the top of her hip bone. I slowed things down to a pace we could both handle. The wild curls of her long hair got caught in the gruff on my face as our heads rubbed together. She nodded her head like she was using the point of my nose to scratch an itch on her cheek and her free hand reached back into my hair. We stayed like that for a few songs, but she didn't let me stay in charge very long. There were times her powerful hips broke loose, vibrating faster than a pull-start sex toy. I knew she was just showing off, but I didn't mind. Who would?

It was getting hot on the dance floor. Layers of sweat covered us both. At that point, our hips slowed and we stopped pressing together so hard. She turned to face me, holding my forearms in her hands. We let some air flow between us, but she didn't wait long before she pulled me in by both arms. As we neared collision, her hands ran up my arms and over my shoulders and behind my neck and into my hair. Our faces hit so hard my lips were pinched by our impacting teeth.

After a minute of heavy contact we took a step back to catch our breath. I leaned in and said, "My name's Mike, By The Way."

"Portia." She pulled my ear close to her lips. "Let's go cool off. How 'bout that beer?"

I took her hand in mine and led her through the crowd to the beer cooler in the back of the bar. The entire place was like a sauna, even when we were well away from the dance floor. I grabbed two bottles from the beer girl, and we stepped outside onto the patio. Summer Nights in the district weren't much cooler than summer days, but, even though the warm air was still thick with humidity, it was a relief from the weather in doors.

We moved to the edge of the patio, away from the noisy mass. "If you don't like smoking I'm sorry. Might as well get this out of the way now."

"Smoker, eh? That's so unfortunate."

"You don't smoke. That's so lame."

"Hey, I've got to work hard to stay this hot."

"I doubt that."

"Baby, I work in a gym. I spend my whole day working out."

"Personal trainer?"

"I train a little, but I mostly teach yoga."

"I have to admit. That's pretty hot. Way cooler than what I do." I let the statement hang. It wasn't so much that I was trying to get inside her head. I was happy that she didn't walk away when I lit the cigarette. I was, however, very nervous about talking to her. It had been a long time since I talked to a girl at a bar and I wasn't sure if she'd really like me after she took the time to get to know me a little.

"And what is it that you do?" she asked.

"I'm a full time student and a full time bartender. Needless to say I don't have much of a personal life anymore."

"Bartenders are just as hot as yoga instructors." She took a sip and leaned on the railing with her arm around my back. "What are you in school for?"

"I'm a Literature major." I leaned onto the railing as well, crossing my arm over hers. "I wanna write when I get done with college, but they don't really have that many options for it while I'm an undergraduate, just basic Creative Writing courses."

"What do you wanna write?"

"I've been working on a novel for the last couple years, but it isn't really much of anything at this point. I'm still trying to figure everything out."

"If you haven't figured everything out in a couple years, what makes you think you'll ever figure it out?"

"That's just it. I've had a couple classes on creative writing, but they only teach the basics in undergraduate. The rest you have to pick up on your own."

"Have you written anything else?"

"A lot of stupid shit for class and a few short stories. There's a big difference between a short story and a novel."

"Well, if you're ever a famous writer you better not forget about me."

"I think I'm more afraid of becoming a famous writer than becoming a failed one."

"That sounds kind of backward. Isn't the idea of being a writer to have people read what you've written?"

"I think I'd rather be famous after I'm dead."

"But then you can't enjoy the fame."

"I'm not big on fame and fortune. I've been poor my entire life. I guess I'm scared that the money would ruin everything. If I'm poor, at least I'm writing for me and not for a paycheck. Besides, I'm not really a big fan of rich people. They aren't very personable."

"Says the guy that dropped the worst pickup line in the history of pickup lines. You could have just come up and talked to me. I was staring at you since you walked in the door."

"I've been out of the dating game for a while. I mostly keep to myself these days. I'm either at work, school, or studying random shit on the side."

"What do you study on the side?"

"Everything. If you ever come by my place you should take a look at my library. It's decent for a guy in his mid-twenties."

"Why don't you show me now?"

I'd been a shut-in so long I wasn't sure how to relate to people, especially a girl that wanted to Take Me Home Tonight. The last time that happened, I was desperate for a real bed to sleep in. This situation was infinitely different. I figured the best thing to do was just let it happen.

"I'm down."

We finished our drinks and I led the way outside to my truck. I was polite and opened the door for her, holding it while she got inside. Once we were on the road, I resumed our conversation.

"So you're a yoga instructor? Is that all you do?"

"I do all kinds of things. I've been in the fitness industry since college, but I've also danced since I was a kid. I've got a couple dancing jobs on the side, and that's where I make my real money. Yoga and personal training are just what I do to make sure I have a stable income."

"You've definitely got the look of a dancer." I scanned her body from ankles to shoulders. Her jeans were skin tight above her calves and her thighs looked like they could crush my waist. Her tiny top was loose around the waist, but I could tell she was lean there, too. Her arms were muscular, but not in any kind of body builder sort of way. They were just toned enough I could see an outline of her triceps when she straightened her arms. Although I already had a pretty good idea of what she'd look like naked, I couldn't wait to find out if I was right.

"Keep your eyes on the road," she said when she caught me checking her out. "I don't want to die before I get some."

"It's only a couple more blocks to my apartment. I think I can handle checking you out while I drive."

"There'll be plenty of time for checking me out when we get to your place."

Her direct approach made me feel a little emasculated. It wasn't like this was the first time in my life that someone had been so straight forward about sex. At the time, I wasn't used to talking about sex in any kind of personal way. Sure, I worked in the restaurant industry and every other statement between co-workers was sexual in nature, but it was different when a woman was talking to me about the sex we were about to have. I was still a little nervous that I wouldn't perform well. I was afraid that I'd forgotten the mechanics of sex. I knew it wasn't that complicated, but it was still one of those things that required some level of confidence.

I've always been good in bed. I'm not saying I'm some kind of sexual god, but I knew what I was doing. I've always liked to compare women to combination locks. They come in all shapes, sizes, and complexities. Each lock has some set of numbers on it, but all have a unique combination with which they can be opened. The best part about the really complex women was that they often had more than one layer of locks and learning each new combination to open them was a new adventure. But cracking safes wasn't like riding a bike. Practice made perfect and I was way out of practice. It was all in how well I listened, not just with my ears, but with all five senses. Every woman told me her combination, what place to touch and in what way and order, but she never told me with words – not until we were really comfortable with one another. Instead, she told me with a movement or a sound or a smell. Sometimes when I hit the right spot she squeezed my arm or bit my neck. Rarely, she'd tell me I was doing it right, but she never gave away her secret. If she did, sex wouldn't have been worth all the effort leading up to its beginning.

Even as I drove with Portia she was silently telling me what she liked. I could tell on the walk from my truck to my apartment's entrance that she liked to be dominated a little by the way she stepped close and made me guide her through the doors as I opened them. I could tell she liked to understand a man as she walked through my apartment slowly, taking in all the sights and the way I lived. Even when she was in the bedroom, she took the time to survey all my bookshelves before she put her purse on my computer desk and walked to the nightstand to take off her earrings.

"Nice library. I hope you learned something about women in all those pages."

"What was I was supposed to learn?"

"How to take a hint," she said as she turned to face me, first with her head and then with the rest of her body.

My fear of underperformance was tearing me apart. My heart was beating so hard I was afraid she could hear it. I was scared she'd realize how nervous I was. But then I realized that her heart was beating hard, too. I could see it in her eyes. I could smell it in the air. I closed my eyes and counted past the fear. Each number from one to three seemed infinitely further from the last, but, once the final number echoed in my mind, I left that fear where I was standing. I wanted to let go of everything haunting me from the bottom drawer of that file cabinet, even if it was only for a night. To do that, I needed something else to become central to my world. I replaced the thoughts of Jess and the book with the image of Portia waiting to be taken. By the time I crossed the room, I realized that pleasing a woman was, in fact, like riding a bike.

We stumbled a little when we collided, but she didn't Hold It Against Me. I grabbed her shoulder with one hand and my other hand gripped her long, red hair. In an instant we were close enough there was nothing between us but clothes and Drops Of Jupiter. I twisted our bodies as we fell toward the bed. Once we were horizontal, I started exploring each and every Danger Zone she had. I took her shirt off so fast she probably thought we were Living In Fast Forward. When she tried to pull my shirt off, I helped as much as possible, speeding up the process so we could stick to Life In The Fast Lane. Her fingernails started a New Tattoo on my back as I tried more and more to crack her open. A tight grip in my hair as I kissed down the front of her body told me she was definitely Feelin' Way Too Damn Good. I made sure to doff her pants quickly, but I slowed down as I returned to her. I kissed down her calves and, once I passed her knees, I traced my tongue along her Stairway To Heaven. There's not enough water on earth to wash away my sins, but there was enough heat in that room to Set Fire To The Rain.

Failing Aristotle

She wasn't the only naked person in the room for very long. There came a point when I felt a dual grip in my pull-ably long hair and I had no choice but to let my head pass her waist, proving she was definitely The Fastest Girl In Town. I submitted while she took my pants off and returned the favor. Every time she slowed down to Dip It Low I nearly lost consciousness. All my fears of failure were illogical, as is the case with any fear. After a little time Rolling In The Deep, I couldn't even remember what I was scared of in the first place. Was it a disappointing lay on my part, or a satisfying one on hers? I can't tell you whether or not she was satisfied, but she rocked me like a Wagon Wheel. Once we got past foreplay, things got blurry. The only thing I knew for sure was that we got loud. If any of the neighbors complained about the noise I'd just tell them I spent the night Knockin' On Heaven's Door.

Portia was awake by the time I got out of the shower the next morning. She was wrapped in a blanket looking over the books on the shelves.

"I thought you just used the books as an excuse to get me to bring you here?" I asked as I got dressed for work. "I didn't think you had any real interest."

"You're absolutely right, but you've been in the shower forever and I needed something to pass the time. You weren't lying though. You really do have a little bit of everything on these shelves. It almost seems like it's randomly thrown together. Here you've got classical literature from Ancient Greece and Rome. You've got dozens of books on computers and electrical engineering." She lifted the book in her lap that she'd been looking at. "This is a thousand pages on geometry."

"You say that like Euclid was a bad guy."

"It's not. It's fascinating. Have you read all of these?"

"I haven't read them all from cover to cover, but I know the information in all of them."

"So you lied to me."

"I didn't lie."

"I asked you what you did and you told me you were a student."

"I am a student."

"No, you're a renaissance man disguised as a student. I've never seen a person study this broad of a subject base."

"But all this knowledge doesn't really count for anything. If you don't have a degree you're not educated."

"Oh, I'm sure you're educated. I heard once that it's dangerous to be a renaissance man in such a specialized world."

"It's only dangerous for the world."

She paused after the comment. Slowly she slid the book she was holding back into its place on the shelf. Her fingers paused at the top of the spine. I could see the wheels turning inside her head. I couldn't know exactly what she was thinking, but there were only a few possibilities. The one I saw most at the edge of her eyes was that she wanted to make me late for work.

She did.

After we were dressed and ready to leave, I drove her back to her place in Chinatown. We traded numbers before I turned around and drove to work. It was a lunch shift, so there wouldn't be a lot going on. During the day, I only got a few customers. Sometimes I got a few tables on the restaurant floor if a server called in sick, but that wasn't an absolute by any means. Most of the day was spent restocking the bar and making sure everything was clean and prepped for the night.

When I got off work, I finally took the time to look at my phone. Jessica sent me a few texts the night before, and she called me at one in the morning. I also had a text from Portia. "I had fun last night. Let me know if you ever want to do it again. I'm not talking about a date, just fun."

I smiled and went back to looking through Jessica's string of messages. She was never great at responding to messages, but God forbid I didn't respond to her. She sent me a message once an hour from eight until midnight. If I wasn't by my phone for her at all times she felt like I was betraying her. I shook my head as I called her up. She was dating someone else and I'm the asshole if I go out without telling her where I was going.

"Sorry I missed your call last night. I was out and didn't really look at my phone."

"It's okay." Her inflection suggested otherwise. "My plans fell through last night and I wound up staying at home last night. What are you up to tonight?"

"I'm off work until tomorrow, so I'm sure I'll either sit around the house and smoke or I'll find a barstool somewhere."

"You wanna hang out? It'd be good to see you."

"I guess we could do that."

"You don't sound very enthusiastic."

"I'm not."

"Is everything okay?"

"Everything's fine. That's the problem. When do you want me to come get you?"

"I'm ready whenever you are."

I turned around short of my apartment. It wasn't that far out of my way to go get Jessica, so I made the trip before going home. I told her I was on my way before I ended the call, but, as usual, she still took forever coming outside. I was quiet when she got in the car. Guilt had really started to set in. I didn't feel like I cheated on her, but I felt guilty for breaking my promise. Moreover, we agreed on full disclosure, a hard concept for two people that had formerly been in a relationship as serious as ours.

"Why are you so quiet?" she asked when we got into my bedroom.

"Nothing to say."

"That's not true."

"Yeah, well, there's something I'd like you to say before I say what I have to say."

"I don't have anything to say that you don't already know."

"Even if I know something I still want to hear it from you. I'll tell you what I have to say if you tell me what you have to say. It's only fair."

"Why do I have to go first?"

"Because I asked first." We stared at one another in silence. I was still holding on to the possibility of a future relationship with her, but I was okay with the fact that she was seeing someone else. I'd grown okay with the idea when I pushed her into the relationship with him in the first place. I drank too much and said things I shouldn't have. I didn't deserve her anymore, but I still deserved honesty. That's all I wanted, but she wasn't going to be honest with me unless I forced the truth out of her. That was how it happened before, and that was how it was going to keep happening.

"I stopped waiting for you last night." I broke the silence.

She knew what I meant. She was the one that asked me to wait for her in the first place. It was one thing for her to start seeing someone else after what I did to her, but it was another thing entirely for me to start seeing someone else after the promise I made. She finally spoke the bittersweet truth. "My boyfriend is back from his deployment. He'll be in town in a few days…I have a boyfriend."

"You were right. I already knew that. I just wanted to hear it from you."

"I know. I also know that's why you stopped waiting."

"Right again. I'm sorry."

"You don't have to apologize. I know it's my fault." Tears were free flowing from a steady face. "I don't even know why I'm upset."

"You're upset because we both want the same ending from this story. It kills me to think I'm starting to move on." For a long time I thought that she was the only person in the world for me, but Portia knocked my socks off in the space of a few hours. Although the thought of moving on made me a little sick to my stomach, it was nice to know I had someone to turn to if I didn't want to spend the night alone.

"It kills me, too. I know we're just friends, but I still have every intention of keeping the promise I made."

"I can't be your friend forever. What am I supposed to do if you marry this guy, be a bride's maid?"

"I'm not going to marry him."

"Then why stay in the relationship at all? If you have no intention of following through – if you intend to rebuild something with me – why do that to yourself, to him?"

"I don't want to hurt him. He deserves the same chances you got."

"I deserve the same chance you're taking with him then, don't I?"

"You do, but I still want to be your friend. I like having you around. You're the best friend I've ever had. I owe you my life."

"I owe you mine, too, but a mutual life debt is no reason to put ourselves through the pain of watching the other love someone else."

"You love her?"

"I only met her last night. I barely know her, but she really is quite the lady." I looked at my feet because I couldn't bear to see the pain in her eyes. "You love him?"

"I do."

"Then I guess we're both finally starting to move on. That's a good thing, right?"

Her eyes glossed over. We both had this vision of me finishing the book and everything magically working out. All in one moment everything changed. Now we were both staring down the barrel of other people. Sure, I'd just met Portia and Jess was in a long distance relationship. It was like we had our whole lives ahead of us, but we got this glimpse that those respective lives could be absent the most important player. Finally, after that long look at memory lane up ahead of us, she broke the silence. "I'm still going to keep my promise to come back to you. I'm just not ready yet."

"I'm sorry I broke my promise to wait for you. But I'll take my second chance whenever you're ready. You just better be ready for forever. You know *the offer always stands*."

Chapter 10

What is it about that little, blinking, vertical line in a word processor? When there are plenty of words on the page to distract the writer, the line can easily go unnoticed, but, when that line is the only thing on the page, it can be a writer's worst enemy. With every blink it says "write something…write something," over and over, taunting the person foolish enough to get caught in its siren's song.

Holt was caught. He came back to his hotel to write, but he spent the majority of the last two hours in his room pacing and smoking and staring at that little flashing line. Nothing was coming out. He lacked so much as an inkling of an idea. He wasted all his stories on <u>Failing Aristotle</u>. He never thought he had that much material in the first place. That was why he based the main character in his novel on Mike. Holt's life was pretty cookie cutter save one or two experiences outside of the norm. His parents were dead, but they died in a car accident. There was nothing interesting about it other than the story that Holt had made his own life without the normal financial backstop that most people have.

Mike's parents were alive and well, and they played a big part of getting him through the massive college issues Holt wrote about. Holt killed off Mike's parents for the sake of building a more literary character. He had to push Mike, the character, as close to the edge as possible for dramatic effect. The real Mike's parents, Chris and Doug, were not big fans, and they made sure Holt knew that every time they saw him. Still, they loved Holt as if he was their own son. They de facto adopted him when they found out he was an orphan. Maybe if they were there to yell at him again, he would have been able to forget about that goddamn blinking line and type something. Maybe they would convince him to write something about his own parents. He typed "I can barely remember what you look like" before walking out onto the balcony and smoking another cigarette.

The blank page was a daunting enemy and Holt wanted to kill them all. He would just have to find something worth writing about to begin that noble genocide. The sea would have been a great inspiration at that point, but, unlike the night before when he could hear the waves from his balcony, the tide was quiet. If his wife was still living with him, maybe she could conjure some words out of him by offering sexual favors for new pages. No matter what, he had something standing in the way of his creativity. He somehow managed to retype the same novel a second time, but the idea of coming up with something original again was far out of reach. He flicked his cigarette off the balcony. "Fuckin' writer's block."

The screen saver had already turned on when he walked back to the desk. At least he could avoid staring at the line. He took his seat. The envelope was sitting on the desk just behind his laptop. He could only see the sealed end and a few stamps around the side of the screen. He had never been scared of anything in the past, but his fearless mentality must have been sealed inside. He closed the screen on the laptop to get a better look. Sera wrote those addresses the day before Holt left for Colorado, the day she agreed to run away with him. She told him she expected him to have a fully published novel by the time she moved out there to be with him. The blue ink had faded since the letters were first formed, and a couple of the stamps had started to peel off the top right corner. The envelope looked like it had spent the last ten years locked away in the console of his old pickup.

He turned the envelope over and set it in his lap with the addresses and stamps down. His finger had just made it under the edge of the sealed flap when his phone rang. He pulled his finger back out from under the flap and reached for his phone.

"How are you?" Brandi's voice cracked like she just broke an extended streak of silence.

"I'm good." Holt set the envelope back on the desk and leaned back in his chair. "I'm in New Jersey trying to get through all my issues. It's a lot to deal with right now."

"I'm sorry that I was such a bitch to you the other day."

"You have nothing to apologize for. I should have been more up front about my marital status. You were a bitch for the right reasons."

Her voice got a little louder and more firm. "No, you were up front months ago that you weren't looking for a relationship. I guess I was starting to look at our...situation the wrong way."

"Either way I could have handled everything better over the last couple months. I've been slacking at work and I haven't figured out where I'm going to live after I sell the apartment."

"Regardless of our extracurricular activities I'm still your realtor. I can still get you in the Dakota, but there's a good chance it'll be sold in the next week or two."

"I'd love to buy it, but I'm not going to have anything left over afterward."

"Then I can find you something else. I don't have to sell the Dakota to make ends meet. I'm still gonna get the fat commission off your apartment. Even if things are over between us, I'm here for you."

"That's good to–" Holt's phone beeped in his ear. "–hear. I've got another call right now. Can I call you back in a few minutes?"

"Don't worry about it. I need to get to bed anyway."

"I'll talk to you soon." Holt switched the other call. "T'sup, Cait?"

"I need you to come over here right now."

"Where's here?"

"Sera's. We just got back from the bars and…I just need you to get over here."

"What's going on? Is she all right?"

"She's fine, just really drunk. I've been trying to get her inside the house but she keeps trying to walk to your hotel. She says she – just come over here. I'm calling all cars on this one."

"I'm still parked over there so it's gonna take me a minute to walk over."

"That's fine. I'll see you when you get here."

He hung up and slipped his sandals on. When he got outside he lit a cigarette and rounded the corner just north of the hotel. By the time he finished smoking he was already turning left at the first corner past the railroad tracks. It was only a few blocks farther and he could see his car parked just off the corner of New York Boulevard. Sera was sitting outside on the bed of her dad's truck with Cait. He was still walking across her street when Sera snapped to her feet and started running barefoot toward him. She nearly tackled him when she threw her arms around him.

"I miss you," she said as she tried to press her lips to his.

"I miss you, too." Instead of returning the kiss Holt pulled her close for another hug and forced his head next to hers. He looked at Cait over Sera's shoulder. "What the fuck?" he mouthed to Cait in silence. "Let's get you inside," he whispered into Sera's ear.

128

"We should go to your place," Sera began as they turned together to walk toward the front door, "Cait's too drunk to drive so she needs to stay here." She lowered her voice and leaned into Holt's ear, "We can't stay in my room if Cait stays here, too. Let's walk to your hotel. It isn't that far."

"I don't think that's a good idea."

Sera stopped and pushed Holt away. "Do you have another woman over there?"

"No, I just don't think that we should stay together tonight."

Sera rolled her eyes. "We'll talk inside."

Cait took a detour toward the kitchen as Sera led Holt up the stairs to her room. She held her fingers to her lips as she turned to say, "We have to stay quiet so we don't wake up my dad."

Holt followed her into the bedroom, but he resisted when she tried to pull him into the bed with her. He used his body weight to half throw her onto the bed and took a seat on the edge of the bed beside her. "We can't. You have a boyfriend."

"But you're my husband."

"I'm the man you're divorcing."

"I love your writing. I'll say anything to get you back."

"I'd do anything to get you back, too, but this is not the time. And you're in no condition."

"What do you mean?" She sat up on her elbows.

"You're drunk and I don't want to make up with you tonight and have you wake up regretting it tomorrow."

"The only thing I regret is leaving you in the first place. I overreacted."

"That's an understatement. My only regret was that I was too scared to come after you on January seventeenth. But either way this is the hand we've been dealt." Holt pushed her back down onto the bed. He pulled the covers out from under her, but she was little help in the process.

"You're not going to undress me before you tuck me in?"

"You know I can't do that."

"Well, I'm not sleeping in my clothes." Sera lifted her legs and threw them to the side. Although she was clearly drunk, she was still able to get out of the bed in one deft move. When she was on her feet she took her shirt off, pausing before she took off her bra. She dropped the shirt to the floor and turned her head, closing her eyes and shrugging before sliding a bra strap over one shoulder.

"I'll wait outside."

"There's nothing in here you haven't seen before."

"I know…but–" He trailed off as he turned to leave the room. The last thing he saw was Sera reaching to grab the bra clasp. Cait was standing at the door, leaning against the frame. They stepped outside together and Holt pulled the door shut.

"Thanks for coming to the rescue. I didn't know what else to do."

"It's all good. You know Sera. She's unstoppable until she gets what she wants."

"She may be unstoppable, but you're immovable and she listens to you. She still loves you so much, Holt."

"She won't remember any of this in the morning. I don't want her waking up with any regrets."

"That's not my point. You did everything exactly right tonight. You're an amazing human being and you're one of my bestest friends. I love you and Mike loves you and we miss you. I'm not trying to tell you what to do with your marriage, but I have to be honest with you. She told me tonight, flat out, she doesn't want to get divorced. What's going on with you two? Does this have something to do with Failing Aristotle? When Phil read it today, it didn't sound the same."

"It's not the same. I rewrote it for our anniversary. I was going to give it to her the night she left."

"What made you start writing again?"

"Sera and I were fighting a lot. She brought up the fact that I changed right after we got married and I stopped writing. She brought up the books and I couldn't get the story out of my head. I thought I could make her fall in love with me again if she read it. It took her leaving for me to realize the root of the problem. I had a secret I forgot I was keeping and it became this growing wedge between us."

"What was the secret?"

"I still haven't admitted it to myself. I don't think it's forgivable."

"Try me. I bet Sera would forgive you."

"When I went out to Colorado, I nev-" Holt was interrupted by the crash of Sera opening the bedroom door.

"Ready for bed." Sera was in a white tank top and Holt's pajama pants. Her hip bones were visible between the bottom of the shirt and the rolled up top of the pajamas. She grabbed Holt's arm and pulled him toward the room.

"We'll continue this later, okay," Cait said as she turned toward the bathroom. "I'm gonna get ready for bed."

Sera took Holt to the edge of the bed. She pulled back the covers and lay down on the far side, making sure to give Holt plenty of room. Again, he denied her invitation, but, when he took a seat on the bed, he was far enough from the edge that his legs couldn't bend at the knees as he sat.

"Tuck me in, baby." Sera lifted her arms over her head so they wouldn't get caught under the comforter when Holt covered her up. She folder her arms at the elbows, running her fingers through her halo of hair. "Or you could just get in here with me."

"We both know I can't do that, but I'll sit with you until you fall asleep." He pulled the comforter over Sera, tucking the edges underneath her.

"I'd like that, and I'll read your book. I know I said I wouldn't, but I will."

"I'd like that." When Sera put her arms back at her sides, Holt rubbed his fingertips in her hair to help her fall asleep. "You should read it in the car tomorrow if you don't sleep while I drive."

"We'll see how I feel when I wake up." She was already talking slower. Her breaths lengthened and her blinks got longer and longer. "Where are we going?"

"On an adventure."

"I miss our adventures." Her head rolled to the side and she was quiet for a long time. Holt didn't stop rubbing her head. It felt good watching her sleep. "You're my favorite," she said as she drifted off.

It had been a long time since that was the last thing she said to him before she fell asleep, but Holt could not remember when she stopped saying it. When Holt heard those three words he realized how long her leaving had been coming. He finally realized what everyone had been telling him for the last few days: Sera leaving him was the best thing that happened to him in years.

Holt stood up and saw Cait standing near the door when he turned to leave. She had already changed out of her going out clothes and was in an old pair of Mike's Navy sweat pants.

"I'm sorry I had to call you." Cait stepped outside of the room with Holt and pulled the door shut behind her. "I would have gone home, but I shouldn't be driving right now."

"And she would have wound up at my hotel. That wouldn't have been good for anyone."

"Do you have another girl over there? I know how you can get."

"No, I'm spending the night alone."

"Don't have any of those famous nightmares."

"I'll try not to."

Holt waited while he watched Cait walk back into the bedroom and crawl into bed with Sera. As he shut the door he turned and unturned the handle to keep the latch from clicking. In an attempt to stay quiet, he kept to the edges of the hall and stairs trying to make sure the aging floor did not creak beneath his feet. Once he was outside and was sure the front door was locked, he lit a cigarette and walked to his car. He drove back to the hotel along the same route he walked to Sera's, but his cigarette was no nowhere near finished by the time he was parked.

He took a seat on the hood of his car, leaning his head back and looking at the sky while he finished smoking. A few of the brighter stars were visible, but most were hidden behind the orange hue of the city lights reflecting off the night sky. Some of the stars he could see were located in the few constellations he knew. Others were strange to him. Although he could detail the life cycle of a star from humble birth to magnificent end, he never took the time to learn anything about the individual stars. The paradoxical nature of his celestial knowledge drove his attention toward one star in particular. He looked toward the Big Dipper and followed the line formed by the two stars on the end toward the North Star, the only star whose name he knew. His eyes narrowed as he focused on the dim light, but he was interrupted before the inkling of the wish in the back of his mind was complete.

"I was wondering where you were." The voice was familiar, but Holt did not recognize it right away. He looked from the sky to the voice and his head popped back when he realized who was looking back at him. Her lightly tanned skin looked several shades darker when the hotel's exterior lights were at her back. The t-shirt and jeans she wore did nothing to complement the shape of her hourglass figure and her hair looked much smaller when it was pulled back in a pony tail. The glasses that surrounded her green eyes made her look like an entirely different person. But, no matter how much different she looked from the night before, there was no mistaking Cat's raw beauty.

"I didn't think I'd see you again," Holt said as he smiled his half smile, "but this is definitely a pleasant surprise."

Her arms were crossed as she took a couple steps toward Holt, looking at the ground as she spoke. "I was supposed to go back to Pittsburgh today. Did I mention that I live in Pittsburgh?" She paused, looking up and rolling her eyes as she shook her head.

"I don't think we really covered that much of our backgrounds last night." Holt stood up and dropped his cigarette. "I figured last night was a one and done sort of thing. You know, each of us using the other to satisfy our respective needs."

"That was the plan." She dropped her arms and rolled her head, her voice inflecting on the accented syllables. "I was just looking for a rebound. That was why I left so early this morning."

"You don't have to explain."

"I'm not explaining why I left. I'm trying to figure out why I'm here now." She stepped a little closer and raised her eyebrows. "I checked out of my hotel, but, when I started driving home, I couldn't get what I read last night out of my head – not to mention the sex that came after. All I could think about was neutrinos and light and nothing. I made it half way to the turnpike and I turned right back around. I had to see you again." She put her palms over her eyes and shook her head. "God damn it. I must sound like a total idiot right now."

"You don't sound like an idiot." Holt took another step toward her and there was less than an arm's length between them when he stopped. His voice dropped as he continued. "I wasn't mad that you left this morning, but I was a little sad that I might never see you again."

"This was only supposed to be for one night," she said, her eyes moving from side to side and up and down and back again as she stared at Holt, "but I need another chapter."

Coming Spring 2014

<u>Chasing Angels and Failing Aristotle</u>
<u>Volume 3: Prophetic Injustice</u>

Title tracks below:

Dirt Road Anthem (Revisited)
Hell on an Angel
Stay
Your Song
Livin on the Edge